DOCTOR WHO AND
AN UNEARTHLY CHILD

D1319158

DOCTOR WHO
AND AN
UNEARTHLY CHILD

Based on the BBC television serial by Anthony Coburn by
arrangement with the British Broadcasting Corporation

TERRANCE DICKS

A TARGET BOOK

published by
the Paperback Division of
W. H. ALLEN & Co. Ltd

A Target Book
Published in 1981
by the Paperback Division of W. H. Allen & Co. Ltd
A Howard & Wyndham Company
44 Hill Street, London W1X 8LB

Reprinted 1982, 1983

Typeset by V & M Graphics Ltd, Aylesbury, Bucks.
Printed in Great Britain by
Hunt Barnard Printing Ltd, Aylesbury, Bucks.

ISBN 0 426 201442

CONTENTS

DOCTOR WHO AND
AN UNEARTHLY CHILD

1

The Girl Who Was Different

A foggy winter's night, in a London back street: the little road was empty and silent. A tall figure loomed up out of the fog – the helmeted, caped figure of a policeman patrolling his beat.

He moved along the little street, trying shop doors, walked on past the shops to where the street ended in a high blank wall. There were high wooden gates in the wall, with a smaller, entry-gate set into one of them.

The policeman shone his torch onto the gates, holding the beam for a moment on a faded notice:
I. M. Foreman
Scrap Merchant.

There was another sign below the first, its lettering bright and fresh:
Private – Keep Out!

The policeman tried the entry-gate and it creaked open beneath his hand. He looked through, shining his torch around the little yard. There were no intruders. Just an incredible mixture of broken-down objects, old cupboards, bits of furniture, dismantled car engines, chipped marble statues with arms and legs and heads missing.

He turned the torch beam on a square blue shape in the far corner and saw with some astonishment the familiar shape of a police box. At that time police boxes were a common enough sight on the streets of London. Inside was a special telephone that police, or even members of the public, could use to summon help in an emergency.

An odd thing to find in a junk yard, thought the policeman. Maybe this particular one had become worn out and been sold off for scrap. There were rumours that all police boxes would eventually be phased out, that one day every constable would carry his own personal walkie-talkie radio. 'That'll be the day,' thought the policeman. Still, the junk-man must have bought the thing from somewhere; it was scarcely likely that he'd stolen it and lugged it off to his yard.

The policeman grinned, imagining the desk-sergeant's expression if he went back and asked if anyone had reported a missing police box. He paused for a moment listening – there seemed to be some kind of electronic hum. Probably some nearby generator – it was very faint.

Closing the little gate behind him, he went on his way, thinking of the mug of hot sweet tea and sausage sandwiches waiting at the end of his patrol.

The catch on the little gate must have been faulty. As the policeman moved away, it creaked slowly open again.

Next night, the policeman checked the yard

again, but the police box had vanished. Later he learned that the strange old man who was the junk yard's new proprietor had vanished too, together with his grand-daughter, a pupil at the local school. Two teachers from the same school were missing as well.

In all the resultant fuss the policeman forgot all about the oddly sited police box. In time he came to think he must have imagined it. Even if he hadn't, it couldn't possibly have had anything to do with the disappearances. After all, you couldn't get four people into a police box – could you?

On the afternoon following the policeman's first visit to the junk yard, everything was normal at Coal Hill School. The long school day dragged to an end at last, and the long-awaited clangour of the school bell echoed through the stone-floored corridors.

As her history class hurried chattering towards the door, Barbara Wright came to a sudden decision.

'Susan!' she called.

A girl paused on her way to the door. She was tall for her age, with short dark hair framing a rather elfin face.

'Yes, Miss Wright?'

'Just wait here for a moment, and I'll go and get that book I promised you. I won't be long.'

'Yes, Miss Wright,' said Susan Foreman obediently. She went back to her desk and sat down. 'Can I play my radio while I'm waiting?'

'If it's not too loud.'

Barbara Wright went out of the classroom and strode along the corridor. At the sight of her, a group of scuffling, laughing children instinctively quietened down and began walking at a more sedate pace. Everyone knew Miss Wright didn't stand for any nonsense.

Someone had once said, rather unkindly, that Barbara Wright was a typical schoolmistress. She was dark-haired and slim, always neatly dressed, with a face that would have been even prettier without its habitual expression of rather mild disapproval.

There was undeniably some truth in the unkind remark. Barbara Wright had many good qualities, but she also had a strong conviction that she knew what was best, not only for herself but for everyone else. It suited her temperament to be in charge.

She went into the empty staff room – most of her colleagues were even quicker off the mark than the children – selected a thick volume from the shelves, and headed back towards the classroom. Half-way there she paused outside another door, marked 'Science Laboratory', hesitated for a moment, and then went inside.

As she'd hoped, Ian Chesterton was still there, pottering about his lab bench, apparently clearing up after some experiment. He was a cheerful, open-faced young man in the traditional sports jacket and flannels of the schoolmaster, about as different in temperament from Barbara Wright as could be imagined. Ian Chesterton took life as it came, going about his duties with casual efficiency and refusing to let anything worry him too much. Despite their differences, the two were very good friends, perhaps because Ian Chesterton was one of the few people in the school who saw the kindness beneath Barbara Wright's rather severe exterior. He was certainly the only one who ever dared to tease her.

He looked up as she came in. 'Oh, hello, Barbara. Not gone yet?'

'Obviously not.'

Ian groaned. 'Oh well, ask a silly question!'

Barbara was frequently sharp-tongued, especially when tired or worried.

'I'm sorry,' said Barbara quickly.

'It's all right, I'll forgive you – this time.'

She perched wearily on a laboratory stool. 'It's just that something's worrying me rather. I don't know what to make of it.'

It was unlike her to confess helplessness, and Ian was immediately concerned. 'What is it? Can I help?'

'Oh, it's one of the girls. Susan Foreman.'

Ian's eyes widened. 'Susan Foreman! You find her a problem too, do you?'

'I most certainly do!'

'And you don't know what to make of her?'

Barbara shook her head.

'Me neither,' said Ian ungrammatically. He looked thoughtful for a moment. 'How old is she, Barbara?'

'About fifteen.'

'Fifteen!' Ian ran his fingers through his already untidy hair. 'Do you know what she does? In my science classes, I mean?'

'No, what?'

'She lets out her knowledge a little bit at a time!' he said explosively. 'I think she doesn't want to embarrass me. That girl knows more science than I'll ever know. Is she doing the same thing in your history lessons?'

'Something very like it.'

'Your problem's the same as mine then? Whether we stay in business, or hand the class over to her ...'

'No, not quite.'

'What then?'

Barbara Wright leaned forward on her stool. 'I'm sorry to unload all this on you, Ian, but I've got to talk to someone about it. I don't want to go to anyone official in case I get the girl into trouble. I suppose you're going to tell me I'm imagining things?'

'No, I'm not.' Ian turned down a Bunsen burner and began washing test tubes and glass Petri dishes in the laboratory sink, stacking them neatly in racks to dry. 'Go on.'

'Well, I told you how good she was at history? I had a talk with her, told her she ought to specialise. She'd be a natural for a university scholarship in a year or two, Oxford or Cambridge if she wanted.'

'How did she take it?'

'She was cautious about it, but she seemed quite interested ...' Barbara paused. 'I told her it would mean a good deal of extra study, offered to work with her at home. The whole idea seemed to throw her into a kind of panic. She said it would be absolutely impossible because her grandfather didn't like strangers.'

'Bit of a lame excuse, isn't it?' said Ian thoughtfully. 'Who is her grandfather anyway? Isn't he supposed to be a doctor of some kind?'

Barbara nodded. 'Anyway, I didn't pursue the point, but the whole thing seemed to upset her somehow. Since then, her homework's been, I don't know, erratic – sometimes brilliant, some-times terrible.'

'Yes, I know what you mean,' said Ian. 'She's been much the same with me.'

'Anyway, I finally got so worried and irritated with all this that I decided to have a talk to this grandfather of hers, and tell him he ought to take a bit more interest in her.'

Ian smiled to himself. It was very typical of Barbara to get herself worked up and go marching off to lecture some perfect stranger on his family responsibilities.

'Did you, indeed? What's the old boy like?'

'That's just it,' said Barbara worriedly. 'I got her address from the school secretary, 76 Totters Lane, and I went along there one evening.'

By now Ian was busily preparing a microscope slide from some mysterious solution in one of his test tubes, head bent absorbedly over his work.

'Oh Ian, do pay attention!' snapped Barbara.

'I am paying attention,' said Ian calmly. 'You

15

went along there one evening. And?'

'There isn't anything there. It's just an old junk yard.'

'You must have got the wrong place.'

'It was the address the secretary gave me.'

'She must have got it wrong then,' said Ian infuriatingly.

'No, she didn't. I checked next day. Ian, there was a big wall on one side, a few houses and shops on the other, and nothing in between. And that nothing in the middle is the junk yard, 76 Totters Lane.'

Ian finished his slide and put it to one side. 'Bit of a mystery . . . ? Still, there must be a simple answer somewhere. We'll just have to find out for ourselves, won't we?'

'Thanks for the we,' said Barbara gratefully. She looked at her watch. 'The poor girl's still waiting in my classroom. I'm lending her this book on the French Revolution.'

Ian looked at the bulky volume. 'What's she going to do – rewrite it? All right, what do we do? I doubt if it'll do any good to start firing questions at her.'

Barbara shook her head decisively. 'No, what I thought we'd do is drive to Totters Lane ahead of her, wait till she arrives, and see where she goes.'

'Got it all worked out, haven't you?' said Ian admiringly. 'All right!'

Barbara looked hesitantly at him. 'That is – if you're not doing anything . . .'

'No, I'm not doing anything,' said Ian reassuringly. 'Come on, let's go and take a look at this mystery girl.'

They went out of the laboratory, along the corridor, and into the classroom, which was empty except for Susan Foreman and the sound of rock and roll blaring from her transistor radio.

Barbara raised her voice. 'Susan?'

Susan looked up. 'Sorry, Miss Wright, I didn't hear you come in.'

'I'm not surprised.'

Susan's face was alight with interest. 'Aren't they fabulous?'

She looked every inch your average normal teenager, thought Barbara. But she wasn't. She wasn't ...

'Aren't *who* fabulous?'

'John Smith and the Common Men. They've gone from number nineteen to number two in the charts, in just a week.'

'John Smith is the stage name of the Honourable Aubrey Waites,' said Ian solemnly. 'It's not so fashionable to be upper class these days. He started off as Chris Waites and the Carollers, didn't he?' Ian Chesterton wasn't exactly a pop fan, but he found it helped to keep in touch with the interests of his pupils, so he knew what they were talking about, at least some of the time.

Susan looked admiringly at him. 'You are surprising, Mr Chesterton. I wouldn't have expected you to know things like that.'

'I've an enquiring mind,' said Ian. 'And a sensitive ear,' he added drily.

'Sorry,' said Susan, and switched off the radio. 'Thanks!'

Susan looked at the bulky volume under Barbara Wright's arm. 'Is that the book you promised me?'

Barbara handed it over. 'Yes, here you are.'

'Thank you very much,' said Susan politely. 'I'm sure it will be very interesting. I'll return it tomorrow.'

'That's all right, you can keep it until you've finished it.'

'I'll have finished it by tomorrow,' said Susan calmly. 'Thank you, Miss Wright, goodnight. Goodnight, Mr Chesterton.'

Ian looked thoughtfully at her. There *was* something strange about Susan Foreman, despite all her apparent normality. Her speech was almost too pure, too precise, and she had a way of observing you cautiously all the time, as if you were a member of some interesting but potentially dangerous alien species. There was a distant, almost unearthly quality about her ...

'Where do you live, Susan? I'm giving Miss Wright a lift home, and there's room for one more in the car. Since we've kept you late, it seems only fair you should get a lift as well. It'll soon be dark.'

'No thank you, Mr Chesterton. I like walking home in the dark. It's mysterious.' Susan put the radio and the book in her bag and turned towards the door.

'Be careful, Susan,' said Barbara. 'It looks as though there'll be fog again tonight. See you in the morning.'

18

'I expect so. Goodnight.'

The two teachers waited till her footsteps died away and then Ian took Barbara's arm. 'Right – car park, quick! We are about to solve the mystery of Susan Foreman!'

2

Enter the Doctor

As Ian's car turned slowly into Totters Lane, Barbara said, 'Park just over there, Ian. We'll have a good view of the gates, without being too close. We don't want her to see us.'

Ian couldn't help smiling at her unthinking bossiness. Obediently, he parked the car on the spot she'd indicated, put on the handbrake, and switched off lights and engine. 'You'd better hope she doesn't! Sitting in a parked car like this might be a little hard to explain.'

Barbara gave him a disapproving look. 'She doesn't seem to have arrived yet.'

'Luckily, the fog wasn't too bad, or I'd never have found the place myself.'

Barbara pulled her coat collar higher around her neck, and said hesitantly, 'I suppose we are doing the right thing – aren't we?'

'You mean it's a bit hard to justify – indulging our idle curiosity?'

'But her homework . . .?'

'Bit of an excuse really, isn't it? The truth is, Barbara, we're both curious about Susan Foreman, and we won't be happy until we know some of the answers.'

'You can't just pass it off like that! If I thought I was just being a busybody, I'd go straight home. I thought you agreed there was something mysterious about her?'

Ian yawned. He'd shared Barbara's concern earlier, but now he was feeling increasingly doubtful about the whole thing. 'I suppose I did ... Still, there's probably some perfectly simple explanation for it all.'

'Like what?'

'Well ...' said Ian rather feebly. 'To begin with, the kid's obviously got a fantastically high IQ, near genius, I imagine.'

'And the gaps? The things she doesn't know?'

'Maybe she only concentrates on what interests her, ignores the rest.'

'It just isn't good enough, Ian. How do you explain an exceptionally intelligent teenage girl who doesn't know how many shillings there are in a pound?'

(At this time, the early 1960s, Britain was still sticking to her uniquely complicated monetary system – four farthings, or two halfpennies to the penny, twelve pence to the shilling, and twenty shillings to the pound.)

Ian stared at her. 'Really?'

Barbara nodded, remembering. Susan hadn't even seemed particularly put out by her ridiculous mistake.

'I'm sorry, Miss Wright, I thought you were on

21

the decimal system by now.'

'Don't be silly, Susan. The United States and most European countries have a decimal system, but you know perfectly well we do not.'

Susan frowned for a moment then said, 'Of course, the decimal system hasn't started yet. You'll change over in a few years' time!'

Ian looked at Barbara in astonishment. 'Decimal system, in England? That'll be the day! I suppose she could be a foreigner. There's something about the way she talks . . .'

'Oh, come on, Ian, admit it. It just doesn't make sense.'

'No, it doesn't,' Ian agreed. 'Nothing about that girl makes sense. You know, the other day I was talking about chemical changes. I'd given out litmus paper to show cause and effect.'

'I suppose she knew the answer before you'd even started?'

'Yes, but it was more than that. The answer simply didn't interest her.'

Ian could see Susan now, looking impatiently up at him. 'Yes, I can see red turns to blue, Mr Chesterton, but that's because we're dealing with two inactive chemicals. They only act in relation to each other.'

'That's the whole point of the experiment, Susan.'

'Yes, I know, Mr Chesterton. But . . . well, it's a bit obvious, isn't it? I mean, I'm not trying to be rude, but couldn't we deal with two active chemicals. Then red could turn to blue all by itself, while we all got on with something more interesting.' She sighed. 'I'm sorry, it was just an idea.'

Returning to the present, Ian said. 'She meant it, too, Barbara. These simple experiments are just child's play to her. It's maddening.'

'I know how you feel. It's got to the point where I want to trip her up deliberately!'

'Something else happened in maths the other day,' said Ian suddenly. 'I'd set the class a problem, an equation using A, B, and C as the three dimensions ...'

Ian's mind went back to the scene in the classroom. Susan had been standing at the blackboard, studying the equation. 'It's impossible to do it using just A, B and C,' she'd protested. 'You have to use D and E as well.'

'D and E? Whatever for? Do the problem that's set, Susan.'

There had been something like desperation in Susan's voice. 'I can't, Mr Chesterton. You simply can't work using only three of the dimensions.'

'Three dimensions? Oh, the fourth being Time, I suppose. What do you need your E for? What do you make the fifth dimension?'

'Space,' said Susan simply.

When he'd finished telling her of the incident, Ian looked despairingly at Barbara. 'Somehow I got the impression that she thinks of Time and Space as being much the same kind of thing – as if you could travel in one just as well as in the other!'

'Too many questions, Ian, and not enough answers.'

'So,' said Ian summing up. 'We have a fifteen-year-old girl who's absolutely brilliant at some things and excruciatingly bad at others ...'

Barbara touched his arm. 'And here she is!'

Outside the junk yard, Susan came hurrying along the street. She paused for a moment, looked round, pushed open the small entry-gate and disappeared inside.

'Hadn't we better go in, Ian? I hate to think of her in that place alone.'

'If she *is* alone!'

'What do you mean?'

'Look, she's fifteen, remember. She might be meeting a boyfriend. Didn't that occur to you?'

Barbara laughed. 'I almost hope she is, it would be so wonderfully normal.' She looked uneasily across at the junk yard. 'I know it's silly, but I feel almost frightened. As if we're about to interfere in something that's best left alone.'

Ian Chesterton fished a torch out of the glove compartment and opened the car door. 'Come on, Barbara, let's get it over with!'

They got out of the car and crossed the road to the junk yard gates.

Barbara hesitated for a moment. 'Don't *you* feel something?'

'I take things as they come,' said Ian cheerfully. 'Come *on*.'

He pushed open the little gate and they went inside.

Even in the semi-darkness, they could see that the tiny yard was so cluttered there was scarcely room to move.

Ian shone his torch around them. He jumped as the torch beam picked out what seemed to be a human body, but it was only an old shop-window dummy with a shattered head.

'What a mess!' muttered Ian. 'I'm not turning over this lot to find her!'

He took a few paces forward and stepped on a piece of loose rubble. His foot twisted under him, he staggered to keep his balance, and the torch shot from his hand. It went out as it hit the ground and rolled away somewhere out of sight.

'Blast!' said Ian savagely, 'I've dropped the wretched torch!'

'Use a match then.'

'Haven't got any matches. Oh well, never mind.'

Slowly their eyes adjusted to the darkness, and they began moving cautiously around the little yard.

'Susan?' called Barbara. 'Susan, are you there?' No answer.

'Susan, it's Mr Chesterton and Miss Wright,' shouted Ian. 'Susan!' There was still no reply. Ian peered round in the gloom. 'She can't have gone far, the place is too small. And she hasn't left the yard or we'd have seen her.'

Barbara moved forward, and something square and solid loomed up out of the darkness in front of her. 'Ian, look at this.'

'It's a police box! What's it doing here? They

usually stand on street corners.' He reached out and patted the police box. 'Seems solid enough.' He tried to push the door open and snatched his hand away.

'What's the matter, Ian?'

'Feel it.'

Hesitantly, Barbara put her hand to the police box door. She, too, pulled it hurriedly back. 'There's a kind of faint vibration.'

Ian nodded. 'It feels – alive . . .' He walked all the way round the police box, reappearing at the front. 'Well, it's not connected to anything – unless it's through the floor.'

Barbara backed away. For some reason the police box made her feel uneasy. 'Look, I've had enough of this. Let's go and find a policeman, tell him we think Susan's missing. They can organise a proper search.'

'Ail right.' Ian paused as he heard the gate creak open. There was the sound of coughing. 'Someone's there!'

'Is it Susan?'

Ian could just make out a cloaked figure advancing through the gloom. 'No, it isn't. Quick, behind here.' He dragged her behind a pile of old furniture, and they ducked down out of sight.

The dark shape came nearer, and revealed itself as a white-haired old man wrapped in some kind of cloak. He wore an oddly shaped fur hat, and a long striped scarf was wound around his neck. The old man paused for a moment, coughing as old people do, and patted himself on the chest. He seemed to be muttering ... He went up to the police box, fished a key from out of his pocket and opened the door.

To the astonishment of the two watchers, a girl's voice came from inside the police box. 'There you are, grandfather!'

'It's Susan!'

'Ssh!' said Ian warningly, but it was too late. The old man had heard them. He slammed the door of the police box and whirled around.

Deciding he might as well make the best of it, Ian rose to his feet. 'Excuse me.'

The old man looked at him in mild surprise. 'What are you doing here?'

'We're looking for a girl ...'

'We?'

Barbara, too, emerged from her hiding place. 'Good evening.'

The old man studied them for a moment. His face was old and lined, yet somehow alert and vital at the same time. His eyes seemed to blaze with a fierce intelligence, and a commanding beak of a nose gave his features an arrogant, aristocratic air. 'What do you want?'

'We're looking for one of our pupils,' said Ian rather lamely. 'A girl called Susan Foreman. She came into this yard.'

'Really? In here? Are you sure?' There was a sort of condescending scepticism in the old man's voice, like that of someone talking to an imaginative child.

'Yes, we're sure,' said Barbara firmly. 'We saw

her – from across the street.'

'One of their pupils,' muttered the old man to himself. 'Not the police, then.'

Ian was alarmed by the half-heard words. Why was the old man worried about the police? 'I beg your pardon?'

'Why were you spying on her? Who are you?'

Ian realised he was being put on the defensive. Somehow it was as if *he* was the one who had to explain his actions.

'We heard a young girl's voice call out to you –'

'Your hearing must be very acute. I didn't hear anything.'

Barbara pointed to the police box. 'Well, we did. And it came from in there.'

'You imagined it.'

Barbara could feel herself getting angry. 'I most certainly did not imagine it!'

As if deciding Barbara was beyond reason, the old man turned to Ian. 'Now I ask you, young man,' he said smoothly, 'is it reasonable to suppose that anyone would be inside a cupboard like that?'

Ian's tone was equally calm. 'Would it therefore be *un*reasonable to ask you to let us have a look inside?'

The old man seemed astonished at the suggestion. He picked up an old painting, and studied it absorbedly. 'I wonder why I've never seen that before. Now, isn't that strange? It's very damp and dirty.'

'Won't you help us?' pleaded Barbara. 'We're

28

two of her teachers – she's at Coal Hill School. We saw her come in and we haven't seen her leave. Naturally, we're very worried.'

The old man was still peering at the painting. 'It really ought to be cleaned ...' He looked up at Barbara. 'Oh, I'm afraid all this is none of my business. I suggest you leave.'

'Not until we're satisfied that Susan isn't here,' said Ian angrily. 'Frankly, I just don't understand your attitude.'

'Indeed? Well, your own leaves a lot to be desired, young man.'

'Will you open that door?'

The old man turned away dismissively. 'There's nothing in there.'

'Then why are you afraid to show us?'

'Afraid!' said the old man scornfully. 'Oh – go away!' He spoke like someone dismissing a child whose antics have finally become tiresome.

'Come on, Barbara, I think we'd better go and fetch a policeman.'

Barbara nodded, watching the old man to see the effect of the threat.

He shrugged. 'Very well. Do as you please.'

'And you're coming with us,' said Ian in exasperation.

The old man smiled. 'Oh, am I? I don't think so, young man. Oh no, I don't think so.'

He sat down on a broken-backed chair and picked up the painting again, studying it thoughtfully.

Stalemate.

Barbara looked helplessly at Ian. 'We can't force him.'

'We can't leave him here, either. Isn't it obvious? He's got her locked up in there.'

They moved closer to the police box. 'Try the door,' suggested Barbara. 'Maybe you can force it.'

Ian examined the lock. He thumped the door, but it was solidly locked. 'There's no proper handle – must be some kind of secret lock.'

'But that was Susan's voice – wasn't it?'

'Of course, it was.'

Ian rapped hard on the door with his knuckles. 'Susan! Susan, are you in there? It's Mr Chesterton and Miss Wright.'

Ian's banging on the police box seemed to annoy the strange old man. Abandoning his attempt to appear uninterested, he rose and came towards them. 'Aren't you being rather high-handed, young man? You *thought* you saw a young girl enter the yard. You *imagine* you heard her voice. You *believe* she might be hidden inside there? It's not very substantial, is it?'

His words seemed to drain away Ian's confidence, leaving him wondering if he hadn't imagined the whole thing.

Barbara was not to be put off. 'But why won't you help us?'

'I'm not hindering you. If you're both determined to make fools of yourselves, I suggest you carry out your threat. Go and find a policeman.'

Ian said sceptically, 'While you nip off quietly in the other direction, I suppose?'

'There's no need to be insulting, young man,' said the old man loftily. 'There's only one way in and out of this yard. One of you can wait outside and watch the gates. I shall be here when you get back. I want to see your faces when you try to explain your behaviour to a policeman.'

'All right, that is what we'll do,' said Ian defiantly. 'Come on, Barbara, you can watch from the car, while I go and find a policeman.'

They were about to move away when the door to the police box was opened from the inside.

Susan's voice called, 'What are you *doing* out there, grandfather?'

The old man sprang towards the police box with tigerish speed. 'Close the door!' he shouted. He grabbed the door, obviously intending to slam it again, but Ian was too quick for him, and grabbed his arm, trying to pull him away. Despite his age, the old man was amazingly strong, and he almost succeeded in throwing Ian off. Barbara came and joined in, and somehow, struggling wildly, Ian and Barbara stumbled into the police box – and straight into sheer impossibility.

3

The TARDIS

Barbara Wright and Ian Chesterton stood gazing around them in disbelief, their brains refusing to take in the evidence of their eyes and ears.

They *should* have been inside an enclosed cupboard-sized space – but they were not. Instead, they stood inside a large, brightly lit control room. It was dominated by a many-sided central structure which seemed to consist of a number of instrument banks arranged round a transparent central column packed with complex machinery. Strangest of all were the incongruous objects dotted about here and there. They included a number of old-fashioned chairs and the statue of some kind of bird on top of a tall column. Beside it stood Susan, looking at them in utter amazement.

Ian blinked incredulously, his mind filled with a wrenching sense of unreality. He heard the old man say calmly, 'Close the door, Susan.'

Susan touched a control on the central console, and the door closed with an eerie electronic hum.

The old man took off his cloak and hat, and tossed them onto a chair. The clothes beneath were even more eccentric (check trousers with old-fashioned boots, and a kind of frock-coat worn with a cravat and a high-wing collar). The general effect was that of a family solicitor from some nineteenth-century novel. Like the statue and the padded chairs, the old man looked strangely out of place in this ultra-technological setting.

But he was obviously quite at home here. Rubbing his bony hands together, he looked disapprovingly at the two intruders. 'I believe these people are known to you, Susan?'

'They're two of my school teachers.' Susan seemed almost as astonished as Barbara and Ian. 'What are you doing here?'

'Presumably they followed you,' said the Doctor acidly. 'That ridiculous school! I knew something like this would happen if we stayed in one place too long.'

'But why should they follow me?'

'Ask them,' said the old man. He turned away to study a row of instruments on the central console.

Barbara looked around the astounding room, and then back at Susan. 'Is this place really your home, Susan?'

'Yes ... well, at least, it's the only home I have now.'

The old man looked up. 'And what's wrong with it?'

Ian rubbed his eyes and blinked – but nothing changed. 'But it was just a police box.'

The old man smiled. 'To you, perhaps,' he said condescendingly.

Barbara said, 'And this is your grandfather?'

'Yes.'

Barbara turned to the old man. 'So you must be Doctor Foreman?'

The old man smiled. 'Not really. The name was on the notice-board, and I borrowed it. It might be best if you were to address me simply as Doctor.'

'Very well, then – Doctor. Why didn't you tell us who you were?'

'I don't discuss my private life with strangers,' said the Doctor haughtily.

Ian was still struggling to understand the central mystery. 'But it *was* just a police box! I walked all round it. Barbara, you saw me. How come it's bigger on the inside than on the outside?'

'You don't deserve any explanations,' said the Doctor pettishly. 'You pushed your way in here, uninvited and unwelcome ...'

'Now, just a minute,' said Ian doggedly. 'I know this is absurd. It *was* just a police box, I walked all round it. I just don't understand ...'

The Doctor was fiddling with one of the controls. 'Look at this, Susan,' he said querulously. 'It's stopped again. I've tried to repair it, but ...' He broke off, shooting a malicious glance at Ian. 'No, of course, you don't understand. How could you?'

'But I *want* to understand,' shouted Ian.

The Doctor waved him away. 'Yes, yes ... By the way, Susan, I managed to find a replacement for that portofilio. It was quite a job, but I think it'll serve ...'

Ian pounded his fists against the walls of the room. 'It's an illusion, it must be.'

The Doctor sighed. 'What is he talking about now?'

'Ian, what are you doing?' whispered Barbara.

'I don't know,' said Ian helplessly.

The Doctor smiled maliciously at Ian's confusion. 'You don't understand, so you find excuses for yourself. Illusion, indeed! See here, young man. You say you can't fit a large space inside a small one? So you couldn't fit an enormous building into a little room?'

'No,' said Ian. 'No, you couldn't.'

'But you've invented television by now, haven't you?' said the Doctor.

'Yes.'

'So – by showing an enormous building on your television screen, you can do something you said was humanly impossible, can't you?'

'Well, yes, in a sense,' said Ian doubtfully. 'But all the same . . .'

The old man cackled triumphantly. 'Not quite clear, is it? I can see by your face that you're not certain, you don't understand. I knew you wouldn't. Never mind!' The Doctor seemed positively delighted by Ian's lack of comprehension. He fiddled with the control console, muttering to himself. 'Now, which switch was it? This one – no, this one.' He looked up at Ian and Barbara. 'The point is not so much whether you understand what has already happened to you, it's what's *going* to happen to you. You could tell everyone about the ship – and we can't have that.

'Ship?' asked Ian, more confused than ever.

'Yes, ship,' said the Doctor sharply. 'This thing doesn't roll along on wheels, you know.'

'You mean it *moves*?' asked Barbara.

Susan nodded proudly. 'The TARDIS can go anywhere in Time *and* Space.'

'TARDIS? I don't understand you, Susan.'

'Well, I made the name up, actually. TARDIS, from the initials. Time and Relative Dimension in Space. Don't you understand? The dimensions inside are different from those outside.'

Ian drew a deep breath. 'Just let me get this straight. A thing that looks like a police box standing in a junk yard . . . and it can travel in Time and Space?'

'Yes,' said Susan.

'Quite so,' confirmed the Doctor briskly.

'But that's ridiculous!'

Susan looked in anguish at the old man. '*Why* won't they believe us?'

'Well, how can we?' said Barbara patiently. 'It's so obviously impossible.'

Susan stamped her foot in frustration, and the Doctor chuckled.

'Now, don't get exasperated, Susan. Remember the Red Indian when he saw his first steam train – his savage mind probably thought it was an illusion too!'

'You're treating *us* like savages,' said Ian bitterly. 'Savages or children!'

The Doctor gave his infuriatingly superior

smile. 'Am I? The children of my civilisation would be insulted!'

'*Your* civilisation?'

'Yes, *my* civilisation. I tolerate this century, but I don't enjoy it. Have you ever thought what it's like to be wanderers in the fourth dimension, young man? Have you? To be exiles! Susan and I are cut off from our own civilisation, without friends or protection, but one day we shall go back.' He stared into the distance. 'Yes, one day ... one day ...'

Perhaps the human mind can only take in so many surprises at a time. At this new revelation, Barbara and Ian exchanged looks of sheer disbelief.

'It's *true*,' cried Susan desperately. 'It's all true! You don't know what you've done, coming here.' She turned to the Doctor. 'Grandfather, let them go now, please, they can't harm us. I know these people, their minds reject things they don't understand. They won't tell anyone and even if they did, they wouldn't be believed.'

The Doctor's face was suddenly cold and hard. 'No.'

'You can't keep us here!' said Ian defiantly.

'Can't I?' said the Doctor. Something about his confident smile made Ian feel very uneasy.

Barbara went over to Susan and put an arm around her shoulders. 'Susan, listen to me. Can't you see that all this is an illusion, a fantasy? If you like, it's a game that you and your grandfather are playing. You can't expect us to believe it as well.'

'But it's not a game,' said Susan desperately.

'It's not! I love England in the twentieth century. I love your school. The last five months have been the happiest of my life.'

'You talk as if you weren't one of us,' said Barbara. 'But you are! You look like us, you sound like us ...'

Susan's face was solemn. 'I was born in another time, another world.'

'Now look here, Susan,' began Ian. He gave up in despair. 'Come on, Barbara, let's get out of here.'

'You can't get out,' cried Susan. 'He won't let you go!'

Ian pushed past her and strode up to the Doctor, who was still standing at the control panel. He gazed down at the maze of switches and dials.

'Susan closed the door from here, I saw her. Now, which is it, Doctor? Which control operates the door?'

'Still think it's all an illusion?' asked the Doctor mockingly.

Ian glared at him. 'I know that free movement in Time and Space is a scientific dream that isn't going to be solved in a junk yard!'

'Your arrogance is nearly as great as your ignorance, young man!'

'Will you open the door?'

The Doctor gave another of his mocking chuckles.

'Open that door!'

The Doctor didn't move.

Ian looked appealingly at Susan. 'Won't you help us, Susan?'

She hesitated, then shook her head. 'I'm sorry, I mustn't.'

Ian reached out towards the console. 'Very well, then I'll have to risk it myself.'

The Doctor shrugged. 'I can hardly stop you.'

(Only Susan saw the Doctor's hand reach out to the console and flick the immobiliser switch.)

Ian reached out to the controls and hovered for a moment.

As his hand came down, Susan screamed, 'Not that one, it's live!'

It was too late. Ian touched the faulty switch, there was a crackle of power, and he was hurled clean across the control room.

He slumped dazed against the wall, and slid to the floor. Barbara ran to kneel beside him. She looked angrily up at the Doctor. 'What on earth do you think you're doing? Ian, are you all right?'

'I think so. Just a bit shaken.'

Barbara helped him to his feet.

Susan was talking to the Doctor in a low urgent voice. 'Grandfather, let them go now, *please*.'

The old man shook his head in childish obstinacy. 'By tomorrow we should be a public spectacle, a subject for news and gossip!'

'They won't say anything.'

'My dear child, of course they will! Put yourself in their place. They're bound to make some sort of complaint to the authorities or, at the very least, talk to their friends.' He paused impressively. 'If I do let them go, Susan, we shall have to go as well.'

'No, grandfather.'

'My dear child, there's no alternative.'

'But I want to stay. Look, grandfather, they're both good people. Why won't you trust them? All you've got to do is make them promise to keep our secret.'

'It's out of the question.'

'I won't go, grandfather. I won't leave the twentieth century.' Susan drew a deep breath. 'I'd rather leave the TARDIS – and you.'

It was clear that the old man was badly shaken by Susan's threat. 'Now you're being sentimental and childish,' he snapped.

'I mean it, grandfather!'

'Very well. But remember, if they go, you must go with them. I'll open the door.' He went over to the console.

Relieved that the nightmare seemed to be ending at last, Barbara whispered, 'Are you coming, Susan?'

But Susan was watching the Doctor. His hands performed a complicated series of movements over the control console, and the central column began to rise and fall.

'No, grandfather,' screamed Susan. 'Mr Chesterton, stop him. He's starting the ship. We're going to take off!'

Instinctively, Ian leaped across the control room, and grappled with the Doctor. Once again he discovered that the old man was far stronger than he looked. With a mighty effort, Ian managed to drag the Doctor away from the console. But suddenly the old man twisted in his grasp, dashed to the console and pulled what was obviously some kind of master switch. The whole control room seemed to spin like a top. Ian and Barbara were both hurled from their feet, and everything went black ...

It was just as well that there was no one in the junk yard. If the policeman on the beat had paid a return visit at this particular moment, he would have seen a most extraordinary sight.

With a strange wheezing groaning sound the blue police box simply faded way.

The TARDIS was in flight.

4

The Dawn of Time

It was a bleak and rocky plain, rimmed by distant jagged mountains. A broad sluggish river ran through the centre of the plain, fringed by dense, impenetrable forest. There were caves in the foothills of the mountains, and it was here that the Tribe made their home.

In many ways they were fortunate. Once the wild beasts who laired in them had been driven out, the caves were warm and dry. There was water from the river, fruits and berries in the forest. There was game in the forest too, savage beasts who provided meat for the stomachs of the Tribe, and skins for their clothing – if you could kill them, before they killed you.

The man called Kal was a newcomer to the Tribe, but he was by far the best of its hunters, skilled and patient and cunning. Kal never returned to the caves without the carcass of some kill, and it was this above all that had won him acceptance.

One day Kal was following tracks at the edge of the forest when he saw a miracle. There was a wheezing groaning sound, quite unlike the roar of any beast. Peering cautiously from the edge of the forest, Kal saw a strange blue shape appear from nowhere.

Many of the Tribe would have fled in terror, but Kal was more intelligent than the rest, and with the intelligence came curiosity. Although his heart was pounding with terror, he stayed where he was, watching the blue shape to see what it would do. Kal wanted more than acceptance from his new Tribe. He wanted power - the power of the leader. He wanted Hur, the most beautiful maiden in the Tribe, to be his mate. And he wanted to kill Za, son of the old chief, his only serious rival.

Kal stared hungrily at the blue shape, tugging at his short jutting beard. Here was something new, something that so far only he had seen. His scheming mind considered the novelty, looking for ways to turn it to his own advantage ... If there was magic here, he would find a way to make it work for him ...

In the great central cave of the Tribe, they were waiting for magic too. Za sat cross-legged before the ashes of a long-dead fire, the Tribe gathered around him in a circle. Men and boys, women and children, all watched intently as Za plunged his hands into the ashes, gripped the charred and blackened fragments of wood until they splintered in his grasp, his face twisted with concentration, his great muscles knotted with strain, as if determined to force the dead sticks to do his will.

43

But the ashes remained cold and dead.

The slender dark girl by his side produced a carved rattle of bone. It was an ancient and holy object, and there was a low gasp of awe. Za shook the rattle angrily at the ashes, then plunged his hands into them yet again. Nothing happened. Za's shoulders slumped despairingly.

A little apart from the rest of the Tribe, a skeletal, grey-haired old woman sat mumbling on a bone. This was Old Mother – Za's mother – the mate of his dead father, Gor. When Gor had been alive and chief, the best of the food and skins had come to Old Mother by right. Now she was nothing. According to the custom of the Tribe, she should have been cast out of the cave to die, but some streak of softness in Za made him keep her alive. Strangely enough, this only made her despise her son the more. Za would never make a chief like his father. 'Where is the fire that Za makes?' she cackled.

The girl at Za's side was called Hur. She was quick to come to his defence. 'The fire is in his hands, Old Mother. It will not go into the wood.'

Za scowled down at the ashes. 'My father made fire.'

Old Mother muttered, 'So he did – and he died for it.'

Za's father had gone hunting one day, and had never returned. Such incidents were common enough. Often the beast was quicker or more cunning than the hunter. It kept the numbers of

44

the Tribe low, and meant more food for those who lived.

'My father died hunting,' rumbled Za angrily.

'Gor was a great hunter. I never saw the beast that could destroy him. He angered the gods by making fire.'

Za stared at her in angry confusion. 'He taught me how to make the sharp stones for spears and axes. He taught me how to make traps for the bear and the tiger. He would have taught me how to make fire, if the beast had not killed him.'

'So that everyone would bow to you as they bowed to him,' sneered Old Mother. But she knew Za spoke the truth. The secret of making fire was the most jealously guarded of all, handed down from chief to chief. Gor had hung on to the secret as long as he could – a full grown son can be a rival, too. He was always promising that one day soon he would teach Za how to make fire – but he died before the promise could be kept.

Now Za was chief, partly because he was Gor's son, more because he was the strongest warrior of the Tribe. But he still lacked the one magical attribute of a true chief – the ability to make the fire come from his hands into the wood. Suddenly, Za leapt to his feet, and loomed threateningly over Old Mother. 'Tell me what my father did to make fire!'

'He crouched over the wood, and moved his hands as you do. But always, he kept his back turned, hiding the wood with his body. I never saw the moment when the fire came. That is all I know.'

'Ah, get out of my sight, old woman. You should

45

have died with him.'

Old Mother rose and hobbled away. 'Fire is evil,' she muttered. 'Gor died because his pride angered the gods. It is better to live without fire, as we did in the old times.' She laughed triumphantly. 'The fire is gone now. Za will never make fire.'

Za was crouched over the pile of sticks again. 'Throw on more of the ashes of the dead fire,' he ordered. 'Perhaps the spirit of the fire still lives in them.'

Hur threw on more ashes, and Za went on gripping the charred sticks, striking them together, willing the fire to come. The girl Hur crouched at his side, her lips close to his ear. 'The old men talk against you, Za. They say it would be better for the stranger Kal to lead us. They say you sit all day rubbing your hands together, while Kal brings us meat.'

'Without meat we go hungry,' said Za. 'But without fire we shall die when the cold time comes again. Without fire, the beasts of the forest will raid our caves when they are hungry, steal our women and children while we sleep.'

'Old men see no further than the meat that fills their bellies. They will make Kal the leader. And Horg, my father, will give me to *him*.'

Horg was one of the elders of the Tribe. He was old now, but he was still a man of great influence. Since he was no longer the strongest, he would support the strongest. It was the law of survival.

'Kal!' said Za moodily. 'Kal is no leader. It is not

so easy to be leader.'

Kal had appeared from over the mountains one day, sole survivor of some distant tribe that had perished in the great cold. He had brought the body of a newly killed buck with him as a peace offering. Kal was a fine hunter, a quick thinker and a great talker. Instead of killing him, as was their custom with strangers, the Tribe had allowed him to join them. It had been, thought Za, a great mistake not killing Kal. By now, Kal had gathered a considerable following, and there were those who spoke of him for chief.

Za knew instinctively that Kal was no fit leader for the Tribe. He was greedy and ruthless, wanting everything for himself. Za took the biggest share of the kill, and the warmest skins, as was his right, but he cared for the Tribe as well, seeing that hunting parties were organised, and that even in times of hardship the women and children were given food. A leader must think of many things.

'Kal is no leader,' muttered Za again.

Hur said, 'The leader is the one who makes fire!'

Za sent the pile of sticks flying with one sweep of his powerful arm. 'Where has the fire gone? *Where?*'

Ian Chesterton came back to consciousness with a bruised body and a throbbing head. Cautiously, he raised his hand and rubbed it over his scalp. There was a lump just above one ear. It was sore, but there didn't seem to be any blood.

A voice called, 'Ian? Ian are you all right?'

He opened his eyes and saw Barbara kneeling beside him. 'This is getting to be a habit,' he muttered. 'I'm all right, I think. Must have hit my head when ...' He broke off as the memory of the evening's extraordinary events came flooding back. 'Well, at least we've stopped moving.' Ian got gingerly to his feet, looked round and saw Susan and the Doctor standing by the central console, studying one of the instrument banks.

'The base seems to be steady,' Susan was saying.

The Doctor nodded, checking another row of dials. 'Layer of sand, and thin topsoil – nearby rock formations ... good ... good ...'

Susan turned, smiling at Ian and Barbara. 'Are you feeling better? We've left 1963, I'm afraid.'

The Doctor nodded in agreement. 'Oh yes, undoubtedly. I'll tell you where we are in a moment – and when!' The Doctor leaned over the console and rapped a dial sharply with his knuckles. 'Zero!' he said indignantly. 'Zero? That can't be right. This yearometer still isn't working properly, Susan.' He realised Susan hadn't been talking to him at all, followed the direction of her glance, and saw Ian and Barbara sitting on the floor. 'Oh, yes, you two!' he said airily, as if he'd just remembered their existence. 'What are you doing down there? You can get up now, our journey's finished.'

Barbara was staring at him in horror. 'What's happened?' she demanded. 'Where are we?'

Ian struggled to his feet, groaning a little.

48

'Barbara, don't tell me they've got you believing all that nonsense.'

'It's true, Mr Chesterton,' said Susan, 'We've travelled a great distance in Space and in Time. Look at the scanner screen!'

The Doctor sniffed. 'That's right, look up there!' He pointed to a small square screen suspended above the console. It showed a bleak and rocky plain, the edge of what looked like a forest and a view of distant mountains.

As Ian stared at the screen in amazement, the Doctor said scornfully, 'They don't understand, and I suspect they don't want to!' He looked at Ian. 'Well, there you are young man, a new world for you.'

'It's just sand,' said Ian stupidly. 'Sand and rocks.'

'Exactly. That's the immediate view outside the ship.'

'Are you trying to tell me that's what we'll see when we go outside – *not* the junk yard in Totters Lane?'

'Oh yes,' said Susan brightly. 'You'll be able to see for yourself soon.'

'I don't believe it,' said Ian flatly.

The Doctor sighed. 'You really are *very* stubborn, aren't you, young man?'

'All right, just you show me some proof, some concrete evidence.' Ian looked sympathetically at Susan. 'I don't want to hurt you, Susan, but it's time you were brought back to reality.'

'You're wrong, Mr Chesterton,' said Susan sadly.

The Doctor sniffed indignantly. 'He's saying I'm a charlatan! Just what evidence would satisfy you, young man?'

'That's easy. Just open the doors, Doctor Foreman.'

'Foreman?' muttered the Doctor, as if he'd never heard the name before. 'Foreman? What's he talking about now?'

'They seem very sure, Ian,' whispered Barbara. 'And remember the police box, the difference between the inside and the outside.'

'I know ...' Ian looked challengingly at the Doctor. 'Well, are you going to open those doors?'

'No.'

Ian looked at the two girls. 'You see. He's bluffing.'

'Not until I'm sure it's safe to open them,' said the Doctor patronisingly. He checked some more readings. 'The air seems very good. Yes, it is, it's good, quite remarkably unpolluted. Check the radiation counter, will you, Susan?'

'It's reading normal, grandfather.'

'Good, good. I'll take a portable Geiger counter, just in case. So, young man, you still challenge me do you?'

'Just open the doors and prove your point,' said Ian wearily.

'You really are too narrow-minded, my dear boy,' said the Doctor, with an air of insufferable superiority. 'You must learn not to be so insular!'

'Have you any idea where we are, grandfather?' asked Susan. She passed the Doctor something that looked like a small black box.

'Oh, we've certainly gone back in Time ... a considerable amount, I think. When we get outside, I'll take a few samples ... some rock pieces, a few plants ... then I'll be able to make a proper estimate.' He looked reproachfully at the TARDIS console. 'I do wish these instruments wouldn't keep letting me down, though.'

'You really believe it all, don't you?' said Ian incredulously. 'You really believe we've gone back in Time.'

'Oh yes,' said the Doctor complacently. 'Without a doubt!'

'And when we open the doors, we won't be in a junk yard in London, England, in 1963?'

'That's quite correct. Your tone suggests ridicule, young man.'

'Well, of course, it's ridiculous! Time doesn't go round and round in a circle. You can't just step off wherever you like, in the past or in the future.'

'Oh? And what does happen to Time then? Instruct me!'

'It ... well, it *happens*,' said Ian vaguely. 'And then it's finished!'

There was condescending amusement in the Doctor's manner. He looked at Barbara. 'And what about you? You're not as doubtful as your friend, are you?'

'No. No, I don't think I am.'

'Good! There's hope for you yet.'

51

Ian sighed. 'Oh, Barbara.'

'I can't help it, Ian. They're both so calm, so certain of themselves. I just believe them, that's all!'

The Doctor stared hypnotically at Ian. 'If you could touch the alien sand with your feet, hear the cries of strange birds, watch them wheel above you in another sky ... would that satisfy you?'

'Yes,' said Ian simply.

The Doctor smiled, reached out and threw a switch. 'Then see for yourself.'

The TARDIS doors slid open.

Ian went to the open door and stared out. 'It's not true,' he said. 'It can't be!'

The Doctor smiled.

5

The Disappearance

Beyond the door was a bleak and sandy plain, scattered with enormous boulders. It stretched to the edge of a dense, impenetrable forest. To the left, low rocky foothills rose to merge with distant jagged mountains. Away on the right, beyond the forest, you could see the glint of a broad and sluggish stream.

The plain was scoured by winds which made a constant, low moaning sound, and the air was crisp and chill. It was a grim, forbidding scene.

The Doctor sniffed triumphantly and said, 'I've no more time to argue with you, young man. Susan, I'm going to collect some new samples.'

He strode out onto the plain as confidently as if it was the junk yard in Totters Lane, and vanished behind the TARDIS.

'Be careful, grandfather!' called Susan.

'Let's go outside and look,' said Barbara. She stepped outside.

Ian moved towards the door and winced. 'Ouch!'

Susan came back to him. 'What is it, Mr Chesterton?'

'Got a bit bruised in the fall. It's nothing much.'

'Come on, lean on me.'

Ian put his hand on her shoulder, and walked stiffly through the door. It closed behind him.

Coarse sand crunched beneath his feet, and he shivered in the wind. The air was cold, but incredibly clear, and in the distance, the forest, the river and the mountains stood out in sharp-edged detail.

'Well?' asked Barbara mischievously.

Ian shook his head. 'There must be some rational explanation – there *must* be!'

In his heart, Ian knew that only one explanation was possible. Everything the Doctor had told him was the truth. With those first steps outside the TARDIS, Ian began to accept the reality of the whole extraordinary situation.

The Doctor popped into sight from behind the TARDIS, looking distinctly peeved. 'It's still a police box. Why hasn't it changed? Dear me, how very disturbing!' Shaking his head the Doctor marched off, disappearing behind an enormous boulder, leaving Ian gazing after him in astonishment.

The Doctor walked on for some way, threading a path between the great stones, brooding over the erratic functioning of the TARDIS. Recollecting the purpose of his expedition, he came to a sudden halt, and found he was in a kind of sheltered enclosure between two great rocks. Deciding that this spot would do as well as any other, the Doctor fished out his Geiger counter, a small leather-bound notebook and a pencil.

Picking up a fragment of rock, he began examining it with great care.

Soon he was quite absorbed in his work – and quite unaware of the savage, skin-clad figure watching him from behind the rocks.

The Doctor's companions meanwhile were making a cautious exploration of the area immediately around the TARDIS.

Barbara came across the skull of some large animal half-buried in the sand, and she and Susan began digging it free with their hands. 'What do you think it could be, Ian?'

Ian helped them to clear the sand from around the skull. 'I don't know. No horns or antlers. Could be a horse or a deer – could be anything.' Ian looked back at the TARDIS, standing blue and square and incongruous, but undeniably *there* in the middle of the sandy plain. 'Incredible. A police box in the middle of nowhere. It just doesn't make sense.'

Susan glanced back at the TARDIS. 'It's supposed to change shape,' she said matter-of-factly. 'I don't know why it hasn't done it this time.'

'It's supposed to *what*?'

'Change its shape,' repeated Susan. 'It's been an Ionic column, and a sedan chair . . . it ought to be a boulder or something now.'

'You mean the ship disguises itself wherever it goes?' said Barbara.

'Well, it's supposed to, but it just hasn't happened this time. The chameleon circuit must be faulty.' Susan stood up. 'I wonder if this skull would be any help to grandfather ... Where's he gone?' She turned slowly in a circle, shading her eyes with her hand. 'Grandfather!' she called. 'Where are you, Grandfather?'

There was no reply.

Barbara looked at Ian. 'You're very quiet.'

'Humbled is the word. I was wrong, wasn't I?'

'I don't understand it any more than you do,' said Barbara. 'The inside of the ship, suddenly finding ourselves here ... not to mention most of the things Doctor Foreman says.'

'That's not his name. Who is he? Doctor who? Perhaps if we could find out who he is, we'd have a clue to all this.'

'The point is – it's happened, Ian. We've just got to accept it.'

'It's almost impossible to accept. I mean, I can see we're here, but ...' Ian shrugged helplessly.

Susan said, 'I can't see him! I can't see grandfather anywhere.'

'He can't be far away,' said Barbara reassuringly.

'I felt strange, just now ... as if we were being ... watched.' Susan raised her voice. 'Grandfather? Where are you?'

The Doctor sat cross-legged on the ground,

surrounded by a litter of his possessions, examining a moss-covered pebble with absorbed attention. Fishing in his pockets, he produced a curved Meerschaum pipe and a big box of old-fashioned matches.

From his hiding place in the rocks, Kal watched the activities of the stranger with fascination. He leaned forward curiously as the creature produced mysterious objects from beneath its skins. The creature fumbled with one of the objects – and Kal saw a miracle!

Grasping his stone-headed axe, he rose and padded silently towards his prey.

'Grandfather!' called Susan again. 'Grandfather!'

From somewhere in the distance, there came a cry of pain, a yell of triumph – then silence.

'It came from over that way,' said Ian. 'Come on!' They ran towards the sound.

It didn't take them long to find the rocky enclosure. The Doctor's old fur hat lay on the ground. Beside it, was his pipe, and his notebook. Of the Doctor himself there was no sign.

'Grandfather!' screamed Susan. 'What's happened?'

'Don't panic, Susan,' said Ian sharply.

Susan began scrambling up the side of the nearest boulder 'I must find him. Maybe I can see from up here.'

'All right, but be careful.'

'Look, Ian,' whispered Barbara. She pointed.

The Geiger counter lay at their feet. Its glass was smashed.

Ian picked it up and examined it. 'That's no good any more!'

'Maybe he saw something interesting,' suggested Barbara uneasily. 'Perhaps he just rushed off to investigate?'

Ian picked up the Doctor's pipe. 'Dropping this?'

'What do you think happened, then?'

'Well, I suppose he could have seen something and got excited and gone after it,' said Ian slowly. 'On the other hand, he could have been – taken. That yell didn't just sound like excitement.'

Susan jumped down from her rock. 'I can't see anything. There's not a sign of him anywhere.' She looked in anguish at Ian and Barbara. 'Something's happened to him, I know it has. We've got to find him.'

Her tone was close to hysteria, and Barbara said, 'Calm down, Susan, it won't help to panic.'

Susan wasn't listening. She stooped down and picked up the notebook. 'He's left his notes!'

'He seems to have left quite a few things lying about,' said Ian. 'Hat, pipe, notebook, Geiger counter ...'

'He may just have laid them all down and gone off somewhere,' suggested Barbara, more to console Susan than because she believed it herself.

Susan shook her head vigorously. 'No, no, no. Grandfather would never have left his notebook, it's vital to him. It's got the key codes to some of the

58

machines in the ship, and notes about places we've visited. He simply wouldn't go off and leave it. Please, we must go and look for him. Something's happened, I know it has.'

'We'll find him,' said Barbara soothingly. 'He can't be far away.'

'What did you see on the other side of the rocks, Susan?' asked Ian.

'Just a line of trees. I think it was the beginning of the forest. There was a sort of gap between them, it looked like a path.'

'All right. We'll try there first.' Ian stowed the Doctor's possessions away in his pockets, putting the broken Geiger counter back on the sand. As he put it down, he paused for a moment, patting the sand with the flat of his hand.

Barbara looked on curiously. 'What is it?'

'This sand. It's cold. Almost freezing.'

Ian straightened up, and led the way round the boulder.

Inside the cave of the Tribe, Hur watched anxiously as Za laboured vainly with his little pile of charred sticks. Beside him the burly, grey-bearded figure of Horg, Hur's father, watched Za's efforts with a sceptical eye. 'Kal says that in the land he comes from, he was a chief, and often made fire.'

'Kal is a liar!'

'Kal says he has travelled far from his own lands and he has forgotten how fire is made. He says that soon Orb, the sun, will remind him how it is done, and he will make fire for all of us.'

'All of Kal's tribe perished in the last great cold,' said Za furiously. 'If he had not found us, he would have died too!'

'What else did Kal say?' asked Hur.

'He says Orb will only tell the secret of the fire to the leader.'

'I am the leader,' grunted Za. 'Orb will tell me.' He stared moodily at the grey ashes. 'I am the son of the chief, the great firemaker. Even though he did not show me how to put flame into the sticks, I shall soon discover the secret for myself.' Za smote himself on the chest with one huge fist. 'Kal came, and I did not kill him. I let him eat with us, and sleep in our caves.' Za's voice rose to an angry roar. 'Must I spill blood to make the people bow to me?'

Excited shouts came from outside the cave. 'It is Kal! Kal comes!'

'Kal brings us his kill!'

Za snatched up his stone-headed axe and ran from the cave, Horg and Hur close behind him.

Outside they saw Kal, surrounded by a crowd of excited Tribesmen. He bore some strange creature across his shoulders and, as they watched, he dumped it down on the flat-topped rock outside the cave.

Curiously the Tribe gathered round, jabbering with excitement.

Za shoved his way through the crowd and looked down at the unconscious figure on the stone. 'This is a strange creature. Why do you bring it here, Kal? Is it good to eat?'

Kal glared challengingly at him, his bearded face alight with triumph. 'Is Za, son of the great firemaker, afraid of an old man?'

'No. Za fears nothing,' said Za, and prodded the old man's body with his foot.

'When will Za make fire come out of his hands?'

'When Orb decides it.'

Kal laughed. 'Orb is for strong men. Men who can make Orb obey their will.' He pointed dramatically at the body on the rock. 'Orb has sent me this creature as a sign of his favour. This old one can make fire come out of his fingers!'

There was an awe-stricken murmur from the Tribe.

'I have seen it!' shouted Kal. 'He is full of fire inside. The smoke comes out of his mouth.'

'As lies come out of yours,' sneered Za. He leaned forward and poked the body with his finger. 'It is only an old man wearing strange skins.' The Doctor groaned suddenly, and Za leaped back.

Kal was quick to seize his advantage. 'Za is afraid of the creature. Kal was not afraid. A strange tree came, and the creature was in it. Za would have run away if he had seen it, but *I* watched and followed!'

With an angry roar Za leaped for Kal.

Kal dodged aside and leapt upon the rock. 'Hear me!'

'Let him speak!' shouted Horg, and Za drew back.

'I *saw* this creature make fire come out of his fingers,' shouted Kal. 'I remembered Za, son of the firemaker. When the great cold comes again, you will all die if you wait for Za to make fire for you, but I, Kal, am a true leader!' Kal pointed down at his captive. 'We fought together like the tiger and the bear. When he saw that my strength was too much for him, he lay down to sleep. I, Kal, carried him here to make fire for you!'

There was a roar of approval.

'Why do you listen to Kal's lies?' shouted Za.

Horg said, 'Za has many good skins. Perhaps he has forgotten what the cold is like.'

'Tomorrow I will kill many bears for the Tribe,' shouted Za. 'You shall all have warm skins!'

Horg said drily. 'I think tomorrow you will still be here, rubbing your hands together and holding them to the dry sticks and asking Orb to send you fire – and the bears will stay warm in their own skins!'

There was a shout of mocking laughter.

'What I say I will do, I will do!' said Za.

'Hear me!' screamed Kal again. 'I say that the firemaker is dead! You are no firemaker, Za. All you can do is break dry sticks with your hands. But I, Kal, will make them burn – and I shall be leader!'

6

The Cave of Skulls

There was a moment of tense silence.

Za saw the leadership slipping from his grasp. He could not use words cunningly as Kal did, clouding the minds of the Tribe. But he could kill . . .

Grasping his axe Za poised himself to spring.

Suddenly Hur shouted, 'The creature has opened its eyes!'

The Doctor sat up, groaning, his hand to his head. 'Susan!' he shouted. 'Susan!'

Susan, Barbara and Ian were hurrying down the forest path, when Susan suddenly stopped. 'Listen!'

'What is it?' asked Barbara.

'I heard grandfather's voice. It was very faint, but I heard it! You heard it, didn't you, Mr Chesterton?'

'I heard something . . . it might have been a bird or a wild animal.'

'It was grandfather,' said Sudan positively. 'Come on, we've got to find him!' She ran off down the path.

'Susan, wait for us,' shouted Ian. 'Come on, Barbara.'

By now Susan was almost out of sight. They hurried after her.

As the Doctor came to his senses, his panic died down. He studied the savage skin-clad creatures crowding around him, saw the heavy, brutal features, the skin garments, the stone-headed axes and spears. He saw Kal and rubbed his head gingerly, remembering how his attacker had sprung out at him. 'Must have wanted to take me alive,' thought the Doctor. 'He could have shattered my skull like an egg-shell.'

The Doctor looked at the burly figure nearest him. He was the biggest and strongest, so presumably he was the leader. 'Where's Susan – ' he began, and then broke off. There was no point in making these savages aware of the existence of his companions. The Doctor fell silent, glancing shrewdly around him, trying to work out what was going on.

The bearded savage who had captured him seemed to be making some kind of speech. Even in the stone age, there were still politicians to deal with, thought the Doctor. He watched and waited.

'Do you want fire?' Kal shouted. 'Or do you want to die in the cold?'

'Fire!' shouted the men of the Tribe. 'Give us fire, Kal!'

Kal raised his hand for silence. 'Soon the cold comes again, and now you have lost the secret of fire, the tiger will come again to the caves at night. Za will give you to the tiger, and to the cold, while he rubs his hands and waits for Orb to remember him!' He pointed to the Doctor. 'This creature can make fire come out of his fingers. Kal brought him here. He is Kal's creature!'

Za shouldered his way forward. 'He is only an old man in strange skins. There is no fire in his body. The thing is not possible.' He brandished his axe. 'I say that Kal has been with us too long. It is time he died!'

As Za advanced on Kal, Horg stepped between them. 'I say there is truth in both of you. Za speaks truth that fire cannot live in men . . . and Kal speaks truth that we will all die without fire. If this creature can make fire, we must have it for the Tribe.'

Daringly, Hur thrust herself forward. 'Will my father listen to the words of a woman? It is easy to see where truth lies. If this old man can make fire come from his fingers, let him do it now, before all the Tribe!'

There was a shout of approval from the crowd.

Za glared angrily at Hur. He knew that she was trying to help him, that she believed Kal's claim was impossible. But Za knew, too, that Kal was cunning. Impossible as it seemed, he would not have risked making such a claim before all the Tribe unless he was confident that he could back it up. And if Kal's creature succeeded in making fire, Za's own claim to the leadership would be gone forever.

'I am the one who decides what is done here,' said Za. 'Not old men and women – or strangers.'

Kal was quick to seize his advantage. 'Perhaps Za does not wish to see fire made. Perhaps he is frightened. I, Kal, am not afraid to make fire. I will make my creature create fire for the Tribe. I will take this creature to the cave of skulls, and he will die unless he tells me the secret!'

Hurriedly, the Doctor jumped up. 'I can make fire for you,' he shouted. 'Let me go, and I'll make all the fire you want.'

Impressed the crowd drew back. 'You don't have to be afraid of me,' said the Doctor. 'See for yourselves. I'm an old man. How could I possibly harm you?'

'What does he say?' growled Za.

'Fire!' said Horg in awe-stricken tones. 'He says he can make fire for us!'

Suddenly, Kal saw his new advantage slipping away. 'For *me*!' he shouted. 'He will make fire *for* me, and *I* will give it to you. *I* will be firemaker!'

Just as suddenly, Za saw how he could turn Kal's discovery to his own advantage. 'If the creature makes fire, he will make it for me, and for all the Tribe.'

The Doctor meanwhile was searching frantically through his pockets. 'Where are my matches? I must find my matches!' He knew that he'd had them earlier, because he could remember lighting his pipe with them. He realised his pipe was gone as well. Had he left them both behind when he was attacked? Or had the matches dropped from his pocket when he'd been unceremoniously carted here over that savage's shoulder. Whichever was the case, the matches were gone.

Za watched bemused, as the Doctor patted his pockets. 'What does he do now?'

'See, he is Kal's creature,' said Kal. 'He will make fire only for Kal.'

The Doctor abandoned his search in despair. 'Take me back to my ship, and I'll make you all the fire you want,' he said hopefully.

Za swung round on Kal 'This is more of your lies, Kal. The old man cannot make fire.'

'There was a tree,' said Kal desperately. 'It came from nowhere. The old man came out of it, and there was fire in his fingers. Smoke came out of his mouth.'

The men of the Tribe were muttering discontentedly. With the Doctor's failure to perform the promised miracle, opinion was beginning to swing against Kal.

Za seized his moment. Pushing Kal aside, he sprang onto the rock himself. 'Kal wants to be as strong as Za, son of the great firemaker. Yet all he can do is lie. You heard him say we would have fire – and still we have no fire. Za does not tell you lies. He does not say, "Tonight you will be warm," and then leave you to the cold. He does not say, "I will frighten the tiger away with fire," and then let the tiger come to you in the dark. Do you want a liar for your chief?'

There were shouts of 'No!' Men began to glare threateningly at Kal.

67

Kal brandished his axe above the Doctor's head. 'Make fire!'

The Doctor looked up helplessly. 'I cannot.'

'You are trapped in your own lies, Kal,' said Hur mockingly. She moved closer to Za.

Za gave a great roar of laughter. 'Look at the great chief Kal who is afraid of nothing! Oh great Kal, save us from the cold! Save us from the tiger!'

Kal saw his hopes of leadership dissolving in the laughter of the Tribe. He grabbed the Doctor by his shoulder, lifting him almost off his feet. 'Make fire, old man! Make fire come from your fingers, as I saw today!'

'I can't,' shouted the Doctor. 'I tell you I've lost my matches. I can't make fire – I can't!'

Za was almost helpless with laughter. 'Let the old man die. Let us all watch the great Kal as he fights this mighty enemy!'

Kal drew a stone knife from beneath his skins and held it to the Doctor's throat. 'Make fire! Make fire, or I will kill you now!'

'We will keep the great Kal to hunt for us,' bellowed Za. 'It is good to have someone to laugh at!'

Kal raised his knife.

'No!' screamed a voice. Susan ran into the centre of the circle of astonished Tribesmen. She stumbled and fell at Kal's feet.

Close behind her came Ian and Barbara.

Ian leaped forward and grappled with Kal. For a moment they struggled furiously. Another Tribesman raised a stone axe above Ian's head. He was about to strike when the Doctor shouted commandingly, 'Stop! If he dies, there will be no fire!'

The Tribesman halted the downward movement of the club, and looked inquiringly at Za.

'Kill them,' shrieked Old Mother.

Za considered. 'No. We do not kill them.'

'They are enemies. They must die!'

Impressively, Za said, 'When Orb brings the fire to the sky, let him look down on them as his sacrifices. That is the time they shall die – and Orb will be pleased with us, and give us fire. Put them in the cave of skulls.'

The four strangers were dragged off struggling Kal looked thoughtfully at Za, and slipped away.

Horg put his hand on Hur's shoulder to draw her away, but Za stepped down from the rock, and took Hur's arm. 'The woman is mine.'

'My daughter is for the leader of the Tribe.'

'Yes,' said Za. 'I am leader. The woman is mine.'

Horg sighed. 'I do not like what has happened. I do not understand.'

'Old men never like new things to happen.'

'In the time of your father, I was his chief warrior. He was a great leader of many men.'

'Yes, many men,' repeated Za bitterly. 'They all died when Orb left the skies and the great cold was on the ground. Now Orb will give me fire again. To me, not you. Just as you will give me Hur.'

Consolingly, Hur said, 'Za, too, will be a great leader of many men. If you give me to him, Za will remember, and always give you meat.'

Accepting the inevitable, Horg bowed his head and moved away.

Old Mother stared broodingly at Za. 'There were leaders before there was fire,' she muttered. 'Fire angers the gods. Fire will kill us all in the end. You should have killed the four strangers. Kill them!'

Za shook his head, looking into the gathering darkness. 'It shall be as I have said. We wait until Orb shines again in the sky. *Then* they will die.'

Arms and legs trussed like captured animals, Ian, Barbara, the Doctor and Susan lay in a smaller cave, just behind the main one. After binding their arms and legs, their captors had thrown them into the cave and retreated hastily, almost as if they were afraid to stay, rolling a great stone to block the door.

The cave was small and dark, and it stank of death. There were skulls everywhere, arranged in pyramids on the ground.

'Are you all right?' gasped Ian. 'They didn't hurt you?'

'No, I'm all right.' Barbara's voice was trembling. 'I'm frightened, Ian.'

Ian could offer little consolation. 'Try and hang on. We'll get out of this somehow.'

There was hysteria in Barbara's voice. 'How? *How* are we going to get out of it?'

'We shall need to be cunning,' said the Doctor thoughtfully. He seemed remarkably spry after his ordeal, already he was busy struggling with his bonds. After a moment he said, 'I hope you can get yourself free, Mr Chesterton – because I can't.' He looked at the others. 'I'm sorry. All this is my fault. I'm desperately sorry.'

'Grandfather, no,' sobbed Susan. 'We'll find a way out. You mustn't blame yourself.'

('Why not,' thought Ian sourly. 'The old fool's quite right, it is all his fault!')

The Doctor looked at the pile of skulls in front of him. He shoved one towards Ian with his feet. 'Look at that, young man!'

Clumsily Ian picked it up. (Luckily, their hands had been tied in front of them.) 'It's a skull.' He tossed it aside, leaned forward and picked another from the pile, and then another examining them carefully. 'They're all the same,' he whispered. 'The crowns have been split open!'

7

The Knife

The Tribe was sleeping.

Huddled together for warmth, wrapped in such skins as they possessed, the cave people slept, dreaming of fire, trying to forget the deadly cold that seeped through the caves – the cold that would grow fiercer, stronger, night by night. Unless the fire came back soon, there would come mornings when the weak ones, the women and children and the old would not wake. When the cold was at its fiercest, even strong men died in the night.

Only Old Mother was still awake. Fire leaped in her mind too, but not as a saviour, a protector. To Old Mother fire was an evil demon. Her confused mind associated it with the death of her husband, Gor, and with all the misfortunes that had come upon the Tribe.

The strangers threatened to bring fire. The strangers were evil, too. Old Mother thought for a long time, wondering how she might save the Tribe from the menace of fire. At last she thought of a way.

She rose stealthily, creeping across the silent

cave to the place where Za lay sleeping, Hur at his side. Za's precious knife lay close to his out-stretched hand. The knife was a long thin sliver of stone, its edge ground sharp. Old Mother reached out for it.

Za twitched and muttered in his sleep, as if suspecting her intention and she drew back her hand. He slept again. Old Mother snatched up the knife, and scuttled away.

Hur watched her through half-open eyes, and wondered what she should do.

Ian was holding his tied hands out before him, stretching his bonds in the hope of slipping free of them, but the strips of rawhide were tough and sinewy, and there was little give.

Susan was searching the floor of the cave for sharp-edged stones. 'Here's another one with a rough edge.' She picked it up and hopped over to Ian, hampered by the fact that both her hands and feet were bound.

Ian took the stone in his own bound hands, and moved over to Barbara who stretched her tied hands flat on the ground. Ian began sawing at the thongs with the stone. 'It's no good the stone's too soft. The edge keeps crumbling.'

'The whole thing is hopeless,' grumbled the Doctor. 'Even if you could get us free, we'd never manage to move the stone blocking the door.'

Ian raised his head, sniffing. 'There's *air* coming into this cave from somewhere – somewhere else beside the door, I mean.'

'So there is,' said Barbara. 'I can feel it on my face.'

'It may only be a small opening though. Don't count on it ...'

'Why not – you obviously are,' muttered the Doctor.

'Of course, I am. Any hope is better than none. It's no good just lying there criticising us. Do something. Help us to get out of here if you're so clever!' Ian tossed the stone aside. 'It's hopeless,' he said, promptly contradicting himself.

'Don't give up, Ian, please,' begged Barbara.

'All right. Come on, Susan, let's look for a better piece of rock.'

The Doctor had been silent since Ian's outburst. For once, he had lost his usual air of complacent superiority. A little sheepishly, he said, 'Don't waste your time with stones. Try one of the shattered skulls. A good sharp piece of bone will be more useful.'

'Good idea,' said Ian. He began rooting in the grisly pile of skulls.

The Doctor seemed quite prepared to take charge again. 'We must concentrate our efforts, young man. We must all take turns in trying to cut *your* hands free.'

'Surely we ought to get the girls loose –'

'No, no, you first. You're the strongest, you may have to protect us ...'

Ian nodded, impressed both by his own responsibility, and by the Doctor's ruthless grasp of priorities. He found a skull that had been split

74

almost in two, with a satisfyingly sharp edge at the break point. Silently, he handed it to the doctor, and stretched out his bound hands.

The Doctor began sawing at Ian's bonds. For a long time he worked furiously. At last he stopped, gasping with effort. 'Susan, you try for a while. My arms are tired.'

'Yes, grandfather.' Susan took the piece of skull, and began sawing busily away.

The Doctor moved over to Barbara, who was staring blankly into the darkness, her face white and drawn. 'Don't think about failure,' said the Doctor gently. 'We shall get free, and we shall all escape from this terrible place.'

'What?' Barbara scarcely seemed to understand him.

'Try and remember how you and the others found your way here. Concentrate solely on that, retrace every step of the journey in your mind.'

'Yes, all right, if I can.' Barbara looked at him in surprise. 'You're trying to help me, aren't you?'

'Fear makes good companions of all of us, Miss Wright.'

'I didn't think you were ever afraid, Doctor.'

'Fear is with all of us, and always will be,' said the Doctor quietly. 'But so is the other sensation that always lives with it.'

'What sensation?'

'Your companion referred to it a little while ago. Hope, Miss Wright. Hope!'

Susan went on sawing at Ian's bonds until she too grew tired, then Barbara took over. All their work seemed to have made only the slightest impression on the thick leather thongs – it was obviously going to be a very long time before they were weakened enough to be broken.

Susan sat close to the Doctor, watching Barbara work. She was dozing a little, when she heard a strange rustling sound behind her. She turned around. In the far corner of the cave was a framework of branches, decorated with more of the ghastly, grinning skulls. The rustling was coming from that corner. To her horror, Susan saw that the skulls were moving. 'Look!' she screamed, and everyone turned round.

The pile of branches was pushed aside from behind, sending skulls bouncing and rolling across the floor. A ghastly figure appeared, a skinny old woman with straggling white hair. There was a long stone knife in her hand.

Brandishing it menacingly, she advanced upon the helpless prisoners. 'Fire is evil,' she chanted. 'You will not make fire!'

Hur nudged Za into wakefulness. He opened his eyes, reaching instinctively for his axe. Hur put her finger to her lips and led him between the piles of sleeping figures and outside the cave. They stood shivering in the night wind. Za blinked at her, rubbing the sleep from his eyes with his fists. 'What is it? Why do you wake me? Tell me!'

'I saw the old woman take your knife.'

'If you saw – why did you let her? She is old. You could have held her.'

Hur answered his question with another. 'Why did she take it?'

'Who knows? Perhaps she has gone into the forest to hunt!'

'No,' said Hur. 'I have thought long on this. She has gone to kill the strangers.'

'Did she say this?'

'She took your knife. She is afraid of fire.'

'You should have stopped her.'

'Kal was in the cave. *Leaders* are awake when others sleep. You must stop her.' Hur paused, looking hard at Za. 'The strange tribe will not be able to show you how to make fire if the old woman kills them.'

'But if I stop her from killing them they will give fire to *me* – and not to Kal. Come!'

They hurried to the entrance to the cave of skulls – and saw the great stone still blocking the door.

'The old woman could not have gone into the cave,' said Za angrily. 'The stone is there. Why do you tell me this lie?'

Hur went to the cave mouth. She pressed her ear to the little gap between the stone and the edge of the cave entrance. She beckoned to Za. 'Listen!'

Za listened. 'I hear the old woman in the cave. She is talking to them.' Dropping his axe, Za began heaving the stone. At first it would not move, but gradually it started to rock, more and more. Hur ran to help . . .

It took the Doctor quite a while to realise what the old woman wanted. She was gabbling hysterically

77

about fire, waving the knife threateningly at them.

'What does she want, Doctor?' sobbed Barbara. 'Is she going to kill us?'

'No, I don't think so. As far as I can make out she's terrified of fire – she's offering to let us go if we promise not to make it.'

The old woman nodded eagerly. 'I will set you free, if you go away and do not make fire. Fire will bring trouble and death to the Tribe.'

'Let us go,' said the Doctor, instantly. 'Let us go and there will be no fire.'

They became aware of a grinding noise from the mouth of the cave. Someone was rocking the stone. There was a bellow of rage.

'Someone is coming,' said the Doctor. 'Quickly now!' He held out his wrists, and the old woman sawed at the bonds with the stone knife until they parted. 'Now my feet!' The old woman stooped and cut the bonds from the Doctor's feet. One by one she freed them.

All the time the great boulder blocking the entrance rocked more and more.

The old woman pointed to the way she had come in – there was a narrow opening concealed behind the bushes. 'You must hurry. Follow the tunnel, and then take the path into the forest. You can hide there.'

'Hurry,' shouted Ian. 'They'll be here in a minute.' The Doctor went through the tunnel, then Barbara, then Susan and finally Ian himself.

Minutes after they had disappeared, the boulder shifted enough to leave a gap at the entrance. Za squeezed through, Hur close behind.

'Where are they?' roared Za.

Hur looked at the discarded lashings on the floor of the cave. 'She did not kill them. She has set them free.'

Za saw his knife in Old Mother's hand, and snatched it from her. 'Why, old woman? Why?'

'They would have made fire,' moaned Old Mother. 'They would have made fire.'

Hur's sharp eyes had spotted the opening at the back of the cave. 'They have gone this way. Here, Za!'

Za headed for the gap, and Old Mother wound her skinny arms around him, trying to hold him back. Angrily, Za threw her aside. She stumbled to the floor, and lay there half-stunned.

Za peered into the tunnel and hesitated. 'They have gone into the night.'

Hur said, 'They have taken the secret of fire with them.'

'The beasts will kill them. They will kill us if we follow.'

Hur went back to the cave entrance, recovered Za's axe, and brought it back to him. She pressed it into his hand. 'You are the leader, Za,' said Hur softly. 'You are strong, as strong as the beasts. You will be stronger still, once you know how fire is made. Stronger than Kal.'

Za looked at her for a moment, then slipped into the tunnel.

Hur followed him.

8

The Forest of Fear

It was dark in the forest.

The path was so narrow that low-lying branches whipped constantly across their faces, and they had to shield themselves with upheld arms as they ran.

The air was chill, though the forest protected them from the night winds. The path was so enclosed on each side and overhead that it was like running through a tunnel. Still, it was a thousand times better than the ghastly cave with its stench of death and shattered grinning skulls. Susan led the way, then Barbara, then Ian, with the Doctor in the rear. As they ran, Ian became aware that the Doctor was falling further and further behind.

He turned and saw that the old man had stopped running altogether. He was leaning panting against a tree. 'Stop! Just for a moment, please.'

'We must keep moving, Doctor.'

The Doctor nodded weakly. 'In a moment ... in a moment.'

'We're not far enough away from the cave yet ...'

'I know ... I know. But I simply can't run any more!'

'Try!' urged Ian.

The Doctor nodded wearily, but he didn't move.

'All right,' said Ian. 'There's only one thing for it. I'll have to carry you.'

He advanced on the Doctor, who waved him indignantly away. 'You'll do no such thing, young man. I don't need your help. I may be old, but I'm not senile. I just want to get my breath back, that's all.'

Ian looked despairingly at Susan. She came forward and said, '*Please*, grandfather.'

The Doctor sighed and hoisted himself wearily from the trunk. They moved on, though this time at a slower pace. There were mysterious rustlings in the forest around them, and the cries of wild beasts.

Barbara moved up close to Ian. 'Are you sure this is the right way?'

'I think so. We want to cut off the corner of the forest and get back to the ship. We came in to the forest at a different place – it's hard to be sure. What do you think?'

'I can't remember, Ian. I simply can't remember!'

There was hysteria in her voice.

Ian put a consoling hand on her shoulder. 'Never mind, we're free, aren't we? That's the main thing.'

They moved on their way.

Ian heard a noise in the darkness behind him and

whirled round. The bushes seemed to be moving slightly, and he thought he heard a low throaty sound, like the purring of a giant cat . . .

'What is it?'

Ian shrugged. 'Just some wild animal or other. Probably more scared of us than we are of it.'

But in his heart Ian wasn't too sure. He racked his brains to remember what animals had been about in the days of the cavemen.

Not dinosaurs, at least, though that was a common mistake. Luckily for man, these great monsters had been long extinct. But mammoths certainly. And what about the sabre-toothed tiger? Surely that had been around?

Cautiously they moved on through the dark forest. They came to a fallen tree, and paused to take their bearings.

'I remember this place,' said Susan excitedly. 'But we didn't go right by it, we went around.'

'That's right,' agreed Barbara. 'The trail passed it on one side.'

'I hope you're both right,' said Ian. 'Because if you are, the ship can't be very far away.' He turned to the Doctor, who was leaning on Susan's shoulder. 'How are you feeling?'

'I'm quite all right, thank you, young man! Don't keep regarding me as the weak link in this party.'

Suddenly, Barbara gave a little scream, and moved closer to Ian.

'What is it?'

'I don't know. I thought I saw something move –

over there in the bushes.'

'Nonsense,' said the Doctor airily.

'I tell you the bushes *moved*, I saw them. We're never going to get out of this terrible place. Never!'

'What could it have been, grandfather?' whispered Susan.

'Imagination, my dear child. Pure imagination,' said the Doctor, but he looked round rather uneasily.

Ian put a consoling arm around Barbara's shoulders. 'Look, I know this seems like a nightmare, but we'll get out of it.'

'We'll all die in this terrible forest, I know we will!'

'No we won't,' said Ian gently. 'Not if we don't give up.'

'Ian, what's happening to us?'

'Look, we can't be far from the ship now. We'll be safe there. We got out of the caves, didn't we?'

Susan moved closer to the Doctor and shivered. 'It's so cold!'

The Doctor slipped off his jacket and put it round her shoulders. 'You're welcome to this, my child.'

'What about you, grandfather?'

The Doctor managed a smile.

'Don't worry about me. All this exertion has made me quite hot!'

Ian came over to them. 'Barbara's feeling the strain a bit. We seem to have stopped anyway, so we'll rest here for a little while.'

Susan nodded gratefully. 'Is there any chance of their following us?'

'I'm afraid there is!'

'That's why I don't want to stay here too long.'

'You don't think I want to linger, do you?' said the Doctor peevishly.

Ian gave him a long-suffering look. 'No, of course, I don't. I think we'll change the order when we set off again. You lead, with Susan and Barbara, and I'll bring up the rear.'

The Doctor bristled. 'You seem to have elected yourself leader of this little expedition.'

'There isn't time to take a vote on it, is there?'

'Just so long as you understand that I won't follow your orders blindly, young man.'

Ian leaned forward. 'Believe me, Doctor, if there were just the two of us, as far as I'm concerned you could find your own way back to the ship!'

'You're a very tiresome young man, aren't you?'

'And you're a very stubborn old one,' said Ian, through gritted teeth. 'But when we set off, you'll lead, the girls will come in between, and I'll go last – that's the safest way!'

'Safest? Why safest?'

'I think Barbara is right. I heard something in the bushes behind us when we stopped before, and it's still with us now. Something's stalking us.'

'Sheer imagination!'

'What makes you so confident, Doctor?'

'I refuse to be frightened out of my wits by mere shadows!'

Ian gave up. 'Very well, suit yourself. We'll rest here for a little while longer, and then move on.'

In another part of the forest, Za and Hur too had paused, though not to rest. They knelt, examining the traces left by the strangers on their passage through the jungle – markings as clear to them as road signs to a modern motorist.

'Here is a broken twig,' said Hur. 'They rested here.'

Za examined a footprint. 'They have strange feet.'

'They wore skins on them,' said Hur. 'There are more marks here, and here. They went this way.'

There was a distant rustle ahead of them, and a low growling.

Za looked fearfully at Hur. 'It was wrong to follow them. We should not have done this.'

'We cannot go back now. Would you have Kal mock you as you mocked him?'

Za took a firmer grip on his axe and they went on their way.

The little party moved on through the jungle, inevitably slowed down by the fact that the Doctor was now in the lead. Barbara caught her foot in a trailing vine and fell, crashing into the bushes to one side of the path. Her outstretched hand touched something warm and wet. Stumbling to her feet she looked at her hand. It was covered with blood. She screamed.

On the trail behind them, Za cocked his head alertly. 'They are very near now. That was one of the women. Come!' They hurried on.

The Doctor was examining the huddled shape just beside the path. 'What is it, grandfather?' asked Susan fearfully.

'Only a dead animal. Some kind of deer, I think. It's been killed very recently, the body is still warm.'

'What killed it?'

'Judging by these claw marks, some very large and very savage member of the cat family – possibly a sabre-toothed tiger.'

Suddenly, they heard a crashing in the jungle behind them.

'It is the tiger?' whispered Barbara.

'Too noisy. It must be the cave people, coming after us. We'll have to hide, and hope they pass by. Quick, over there in the bushes.' Ian thrust them into the bushes, and they crouched down, waiting.

Seconds later, two skin-clad figures ran into the clearing, and paused, looking around them.

One was a massive figure carrying a stone-headed axe – one of the men they had seen at the cave.

The figure beside him was both smaller and slighter. To his astonishment, Ian saw that it was a girl.

The two savage figures stood poised, peering around them suspiciously.

Close by in the bushes, the great cat was also

poised. It had followed this strange prey through the forest for quite some way.

Several times it had crouched to spring and bring one of them down, but each time something had held it back. There was something very wrong about these creatures. Their appearance, the way they crashed boldly through the jungle, and above all the alien smell of the strange skins they wore, all this was new, unknown – and possibly dangerous.

When Za and Hur moved into the clearing, the great beast's dilemma was resolved. It knew the cave people of old, knew the way they looked and moved and smelt, knew how they hunted with spears and axes.

Lashing its tail, the tiger snaked through the forest towards the two newcomers.

In the clump of bushes, Ian whispered, 'Keep down all of you. Not a sound!'

Za looked round uneasily, sensing rather than seeing something wrong.

He touched Hur's arm. 'Wait here,' he whispered. 'There is danger in this place. I will go and look.'

Za moved cautiously into the clearing, heading straight for the bushes where Ian and his companions were hiding. From somewhere behind him, there came a low growl.

Za swung round. It was the voice of the tiger, the long-toothed one, the old enemy of his people.

Granto the clearing, heading straight for the

bushes where Ian and his companions were hiding. From somewhere behind him, there came a low growl.

Za swung round. It was the voice of the tiger, the long-toothed one, the old enemy of his people.

Grasping his axe tighter, Za swung his head from one side to the other, listening, sensing.

Just behind him the long grasses began to ripple. Hur saw it and screamed a warning, but it was too late. The tiger sprang.

9

Ambush

As the tiger hurtled through the air towards him, Za seized his only possible chance. He ran, not back but forwards, under the attacking beast, and swung his great stone axe with all his strength at the creature's side.

He felt the axe-head thud home. The tiger screamed in rage and pain. Its whole weight dropped full upon him, bearing him to the ground.

Za tried to wrench back his axe for a killing blow at the skull, but only the handle came free. The axe was broken ...

To the Doctor and the others, everything seemed to happen in a blinding flurry of speed. They saw the great beast spring, bearing the caveman to the ground. They heard the tiger scream ...

In a flash of yellow fur, it broke free and disappeared into the forest, leaving the blood-covered form of the caveman stretched out in the moonlit clearing.

The girl gave a great cry of grief, and ran to kneel beside him.

Ian jumped to his feet. 'Quick, now's our chance. Get away all of you. Run!'

Instinctively, the others obeyed him. All except Barbara, who stood looking back at the two figures.

'What are you waiting for?' shouted the Doctor.

'We can't just leave them!'

'My dear Miss Wright, they are savages. They would cheerfully have killed *us*. Remember the skulls in the cave.'

'I don't care what they've done, they're still human beings.' Barbara began walking across the clearing to where the sobbing girl knelt by the motionless body of the man. 'I think he's dead. There isn't any danger.'

'Barbara, come back,' shouted Ian running after her. 'This is our chance to escape.'

'I'll come with you, Barbara,' called Susan. She moved to follow, but the Doctor caught her arm. 'You will do no such thing, Susan. Stay where you are. We're going back to the ship!'

'No, grandfather,' said Susan defiantly. 'We can't leave her here alone.'

The Doctor looked across the clearing and said exasperatedly, 'What are they doing? Are they out of their minds?'

Crouched protectively over Za, Hur looked up fiercely as Barbara and Ian approached. 'Keep away!'

'Let me look at him,' said Ian.

'No. You will kill him.'

Gently Barbara pulled Hur aside, as Ian knelt beside Za's body.

'It's all right,' said Ian. 'I'm your friend.'

Hur looked at him in amazement. 'Friend?'

'I shall need some water.'

'Water?'

'Get me some water,' said Ian patiently. 'For his wounds.'

Hur pointed. 'There is a stream – over there.'

'Show me,' said Barbara firmly, as though addressing a reluctant pupil. 'Give me your handkerchief, will you, Ian?'

Muttering and grumbling, the Doctor allowed Susan to lead him over. 'It's all right, grandfather,' said Susan soothingly. It's quite safe now.'

The Doctor snorted in disgust.

Susan looked down at the caveman. 'How is he, Ian? Is he dead?'

'Far from it,' said Ian. 'In fact, he's a lot better than he looks.' He picked up the haft of Za's axe. 'I imagine he must have left his axe-head in the tiger.'

Barbara and Hur came back into the clearing. Barbara gave Ian his water-soaked handkerchief, and Hur carried more water in a folded leaf.

Ian began washing away the blood from Za's wounds, which were soon revealed to be no more than a series of deep slashes in his arm and shoulder. 'Most of this blood is the tiger's,' said Ian.

Barbara pointed. 'Look, there's a cut in his forehead – the tiger must have stunned him.'

Ian bathed the cut, and Za moaned and stirred.

Ian looked ruefully at Barbara. 'We seemed to have missed our chance of getting away. I bet your flat must be just littered with stray cats and dogs.'

'They're human beings, Ian,' said Barbara again.

'All right, I know.'

Ian looked up at the Doctor, who stood scowling down at them. 'Have you got medical supplies in the ship? Antiseptic?'

'This is preposterous,' spluttered the Doctor. 'One moment we are desperately trying to get away from these savages and now –'

'Now we're helping them! I know. You're a Doctor. Do something.'

'I am not a Doctor of medicine, young man.'

'Grandfather, we should make friends with them,' urged Susan. 'Maybe they'll help us.'

'Ridiculous!'

'Why?' said Barbara angrily. 'Why must you treat everyone and everything as less important than yourself?'

The Doctor looked severely at her. 'I suppose you think that everything you do is reasonable, and everything I do is inhuman. But suppose your judgement's wrong, not mine? If these two savages can follow us, so can their fellows. The whole Tribe may be upon us at any moment!'

'The Tribe sleeps,' said Hur.

'And the old woman who set us free, mm? What about her?'

'You're right, Doctor. We're too exposed here.' The Doctor nodded complacently – but his expression changed rapidly when Ian went on, 'We'll make a stretcher and carry him with us!'

'You're not proposing to take him back to the ship?'

'We can make the stretcher with our coats,' said Ian briskly. 'Barbara, Susan, see if you can break off a couple of long straight branches from those bushes.'

As she moved away, Barbara said, 'Maybe the old woman won't give us away. She helped us, she won't want the others to know.'

'Do you think these people have logic and reason,' said the Doctor furiously. 'Can't you see, their minds change as rapidly as night follows day. She may well be telling the entire Tribe at this very moment ...'

Sometime in the night Kal woke, warned by some instinct of danger. He looked around him. Everything seemed normal. Then he saw that Old Mother was gone. And Za and Hur ... Something was happening. Whatever it was, it must be concerned with the strangers. Za had betrayed him, he was trying to force the strangers to give *him* the secret of the fire.

Kal rose, knife in hand, and made his way stealthily to the cave of skulls. His suspicions were confirmed, when he saw that the great stone had been moved aside.

He slipped through the gap and saw to his astonishment that the cave held no strangers, and no Za. Only Old Mother lay moaning on the ground.

Kal dragged her to her feet. 'The strange

93

creatures – where are they?'

'They have gone,' said Old Mother, a gleam of triumph in her eyes.

'How did they move the stone?'

'Za moved it.'

'Za has gone with them? Tell me, old woman, tell me!'

The old woman pointed to the back of the cave. 'Za and Hur went after the strangers. Through there. There is another way.'

'The strangers' hands and feet were bound,' said Kal fiercely. 'Za set them free! They have gone with Za to show him how to make fire.'

'*I* set them free,' said Old Mother proudly. 'Now they will not make fire any more. There will be no more fire!'

'You freed them?' Kal saw an end to all his hopes – the secret of fire lost, or given to Za – and all because of this meddling old woman. 'You freed them?'

A surge of blind rage swept through him, and suddenly the stone knife in his hand was buried in Old Mother's heart.

The old woman stared disbelievingly down at the knife for a moment, then fell dead at his feet.

Kal plucked out the knife, wet with the old woman's blood, and thrust it beneath his skins. He would have to think of something to tell the Tribe.

Ian was busy showing Susan and Barbara how to make an improvised stretcher. 'The poles go through the sleeves of the coats like that you see . . .'

Susan knelt to wipe Za's forehead, but Hur thrust her rudely away. 'No. He is mine.'

'I was only trying to help him.'

Ian smiled. 'I think she's jealous of you, Susan.'

Baffled, Hur looked around the group. 'I do not understand any of you. You are like a mother with a baby. Za is your enemy. Why do you not kill him?'

Ian said, 'These people just don't understand kindness or friendship. See if you can explain, in a way she'll understand, Barbara.'

'We will make him well again,' said Barbara gently. 'We will teach you how fire is made. All we ask in return is that you show us the way back to our own cave.'

A feeble voice from the ground said, 'Listen to them, Hur. They speak truth. They did not kill me.' By now Za was conscious, though still dazed.

'I'm getting worried about the time,' said Ian. 'We've been here far too long. Are we all ready?'

'I'm terribly thirsty,' said Susan. 'Can I just go and get a drink?'

Ian nodded, and Susan went over to Hur and said hopefully, 'Water?'

Hur led the way to the stream and Susan followed.

'Be careful!' called Barbara.

Susan looked at the Doctor, who was standing a little apart, sulking. 'Do you want some water, grandfather?'

'No, I do not!'

'What about giving us a hand here, Doctor?' called Ian.

The Doctor folded his arms and turned his back.

'Don't take any notice of him,' said Susan over her shoulder. 'He's often like this, especially when he doesn't get his own way!'

Ian finished checking over the stretcher. It would have to be pretty solid to carry Za's weight.

'Maybe it was a good idea making friends with these two,' said Barbara hopefully. 'We might even stand a better chance of getting back to the ship.'

Ian looked up from his task and saw that the Doctor had picked up a heavy pointed stone and was advancing stealthily towards Za.

He sprang up and gripped the Doctor's wrist. 'What are you doing?'

'Let go of me,' said the Doctor indignantly. 'I was just going to ask him to draw some kind of map on the ground, to show us the way back to the TARDIS.'

Ian looked narrowly at the old man. Just how much ruthlessness was the Doctor capable of, if he felt it might save his own and Susan's life?

He took the stone from the Doctor's hand and tossed it aside. 'It's a good idea, Doctor, but I don't think he's in a fit state to draw any maps. We'd better get going.'

Susan and Hur were back from the stream by now, and the Doctor looked on scornfully, while Ian and the three girls struggled to roll Za onto the stretcher. They managed it at last.

'Will you take one end, please, Doctor?' said Ian.

'You surely don't expect me to carry him?'

'You surely don't expect one of the girls to do it?'

said Ian blandly. 'Lead the way please, Susan.'

Fuming, the Doctor picked up his end of the stretcher, Ian took the other, and the little party set off.

Kal had roused the rest of the Tribe, and they were milling about confusedly outside the main cave. 'The strangers have gone,' shouted Kal. 'Za and Hur have gone with them. We must go after them and bring them back.'

'Hur would not help the strangers to escape,' said Horg.

'She has gone with them all the same.'

Horg shook his head in puzzlement. 'Where is Old Mother? Has she gone with them too?'

'She sits silent in the cave of skulls,' said Kal. 'I saw her there, but she would not move or speak.'

Horg led the way to the cave of skulls and they all crowded inside.

Old Mother sat cross-legged, staring into space, leaning against a pyramid of skulls.

'She will tell you what happened,' said Kal. 'Ask her.'

Horg reached out and touched Old Mother on the shoulder. She tipped over sideways, and fell stiffly to the ground. 'She is dead.'

In a loud, compelling voice Kal said, 'My eyes tell me what happened here. I see pictures as I do when I sleep. Za and Hur came here to free the strangers, so that they could steal the secret of fire for themselves. Old Mother tried to stop them, and Za killed her. Za has gone with them. He is taking them back to their own tree in return for the secret.'

Horg said slowly, 'The old woman is dead. Za and the strangers are gone. It must have been as your eyes saw it.'

'I am your leader now,' shouted Kal. 'Follow me, and I will lead you to the strangers!'

It was Susan who reached the edge of the forest first. Pushing her way through a screen of bushes, she peered out onto the darkened plain and shouted, 'There! Over there! I can see the TARDIS!'

The others plodded slowly after her along the path. Carrying the weight of Za had slowed them down to a crawl. Frequent rests had been necessary, and it had taken them an incredibly long time to reach the edge of the forest. But they were here at last, and safety was in sight.

'Come on, Doctor,' shouted Ian. 'We're nearly there, just one final effort.'

'Yes, yes, very well,' grumbled the Doctor.

'Barbara, you and Susan hold back the bushes so we can get the stretcher through,' said Ian.

Barbara and Susan pulled the screen of bushes aside, and Ian led the way through the gap with the stretcher. As he came out onto the plain, he could make out the square blue shape of the TARDIS just ahead.

Suddenly, to his horror, he saw a number of burly, skin-clad figures emerge from behind the TARDIS and advance towards them.

'Back!' shouted Ian. He retreated clumsily back into the forest, hampered by the stretcher, swung round and saw another group of tribesmen blocking the path.

The leader had a short jutting beard, and there was a stone knife in his hand.

They were trapped.

10

Captured

The Tribe was holding a council.

The four recaptured prisoners stood before Horg and the rest of the Tribe, guarded by a circle of warriors, led by Kal. Za was there too, still on his improvised stretcher, which had been placed on the ground before the flat-topped rock. Hur knelt anxiously beside him. A kind of trial was taking place, with Kal accusing Za, and justifying his own actions to the Tribe.

The Doctor and the others watched carefully, realising that their own fates were probably at stake as well.

Kal was concluding his story. 'Za and the woman were going with the strangers – with our enemies! I led the others and we stopped them, brought them back here.'

'The strangers are not our enemies,' said Hur. 'They saved Za from death when the tiger attacked him by the stream.'

'Hear the woman speak for the strangers,' sneered Kal. 'She and Za let them out of the cave of skulls, and fled with them.'

'You lie,' shouted Hur. 'Old Mother set them free.'

'Is Za so weak that his woman must speak for him?'

'I say it was Old Mother! She showed them another way from the cave of skulls. She will tell you!'

'The old woman speaks no more,' said Kal. 'She does not say she did this, or did that. Old Mother is dead. Za killed her.'

Kal stooped and snatched the stone knife from beneath Za's skins. 'See! Here is the knife Za killed her with!'

There was a rumble of anger from the Tribe.

Suddenly, the Doctor spoke, his voice loud and commanding. 'The knife has no blood on it.'

Everyone stared at the knife. As the Doctor had said, the stone blade was clean.

Kal looked down at the knife in his hand. 'It is a bad knife! It does not show the things it has done.'

The Doctor laughed scornfully. 'It is a finer knife than yours.'

Kal hurled the knife to the ground. 'I say it is a bad knife.'

The Doctor pointed to the knife where it lay on the ground. 'I say this is a fine knife. It can cut and it can stab. It is a knife for a chief. I have never seen a better knife than this.'

'I will show you one!' Kal snatched out his own knife and held it out. It was a fine knife indeed – and the blade was caked with dried blood.

The Doctor's voice rang out. 'Your knife shows

the things that it has done. Your knife has blood on it! Who killed the old woman?'

Za raised himself on one elbow. 'I did not kill her.' He struggled to his feet, and stood swaying to and fro a moment. 'Kal killed her!'

'The old woman set the strangers free,' screamed Kal. 'She showed the the way to leave the cave of skulls without moving the great stone. I, Kal, killed her!'

The Doctor stepped forward, spreading out his hands. In some extraordinary way he was dominating the whole savage gathering. 'Is this your strong leader? One who kills your old women in his fury? He is a bad leader. He will kill you all when he is angry.' He leaned across to Ian and spoke in his normal voice. 'Follow my example, young man!'

The Doctor bent and picked up a stone and hurled it at Kal. 'Drive him out!'

Kal gave a roar of anger, and brandished his knife.

Ian, too, grabbed a stone and flung it at Kal. 'Yes, drive him out. He kills old women!'

Hur snatched up a stone and threw it. 'Kal is evil! Drive him out!'

Reeling a little, Za bent and picked up a stone. 'Drive him out!'

Suddenly, everyone was picking up stones and throwing them. Kal stood helplessly for a moment in the hail of missiles, and then turned and fled into the darkness.

'Well done, Doctor,' whispered Barbara.

The Doctor gave her a self-satisfied smirk.

'Child's play, my dear. These people are just as susceptible to mass hysteria as the people of your own time.'

The victory over Kal seemed to have given Za back his strength. 'Kal is no longer of this Tribe,' he shouted. 'We will watch for him. If he comes back we will kill him.'

Hur said anxiously, 'Kal is strong, and you are weak from your wounds. He will kill you if he can.'

'Remember,' said Ian. 'Kal is not stronger than the whole Tribe.'

Za looked hard at Ian, as if struggling to understand the new idea. At last he nodded, pleased. 'We will *all* fight Kal, if he comes back.' Za pointed to one of the young warriors. 'You will watch for him!'

The warrior nodded and moved away from the cave, looking in the direction in which Kal had fled.

His authority restored, Za turned to the other warriors. 'Return the prisoners to the cave of skulls.'

Ian sprang forward. 'No, Za. I am your friend. Take us to the place where Kal found us, and I will make fire for you.'

Za ignored him, selecting other Tribesmen. 'We shall use the great stone to close the cave again, and you will stand by another place that I will show you.' He raised his voice. 'Take them away!'

Tribesmen descended on the Doctor, Susan, Ian and Barbara, gripping their arms.

'Don't struggle,' called the Doctor. Rather

103

unnecessarily, thought Ian, since struggle against their brutish captors would have been quite useless.

They were dragged away.

Za watched them thrust into the cave and saw the stone rolled tight against the entrance. He turned to a warrior and led him to a clump of bushes not far from the cave. 'The other way out of the cave leads here. If you see them come out – kill them.'

In the cave of skulls, the Doctor and his companions stood looking around them in despair. A hazardous escape, a long and dangerous journey, and now they were back where they had started, in this terrible cave with its piles of rotting skulls and its cloying stench of death.

Barbara saw the body of Old Mother at the back of the cave and gave a scream of horror. 'This place is evil,' she sobbed. 'Evil!'

'At least they haven't tied our hands this time. Well, Doctor, what do we do now? Got any bright ideas?'

The Doctor stood lost in thought, rubbing his chin. He looked up. 'As a matter of fact, young man – I have!'

Za and Hur were talking, standing by the flat stone in front of the great cave. Za was almost himself again by now. The claw marks on his arm and shoulder had stopped bleeding, and he was able to ignore them. His mind was full of questions.

'Tell me what happened after I fought with the

beast in the forest.'

'You were stronger than the beast,' said Hur proudly. 'It took away your axe-head in its side. You lay on the earth, covered with the blood of the beast. I thought you were dead.'

'And the strangers? Tell me what they did!'

'The young man of their tribe came towards you. He did not kill you. He told me his name.'

'His name?'

'He said his name was Friend.'

'They must have come from the other side of the mountains,' said Za thoughtfully.

'But nothing lives there.'

'So we thought. But I see that we were wrong. This new tribe comes from there. Tell me more of what happened. Tell me what the strangers did next.'

Hur frowned, struggling to remember. 'I did not understand them, Za. They moved slowly, and their faces were not fierce. They cared for your wounds, and carried you on their skins, as a mother carries her baby. Why did they not kill us, Za? We were their enemies. We made them captive.'

Za shrugged helplessly. 'They are a new tribe. They are not like us. Not like Kal's tribe either. Their minds hold strange thoughts. The young one, the one called Friend, spoke strange words to us.'

'I do not remember.'

Za frowned with the effort of recollection. 'He said, "Kal is not stronger than the whole Tribe."'

'I do not understand.'

'It is a new thought,' said Za. 'But I understand. Except for me, Kal is the strongest warrior in the whole Tribe. And I was weak. But the whole Tribe drove Kal away with the stones. Even the old men and women, even the children, were stronger than Kal, *together*.'

Za wrestled with this new concept of co-operation. 'The whole Tribe can gather more fruit than one. The whole Tribe can kill the beasts in the forest, where just one hunter would die.'

'Their minds are not like ours,' agreed Hur. 'Perhaps they come from Orb. That is what the old men are saying. They say we must return them to Orb in sacrifice.'

'No, they come from a tribe across the mountains. They can make fire, but they do not want to tell us, because our Tribe would become as strong as theirs.'

'What will you do with the strangers, Za? Will you kill them?'

Za shook his head. 'Your father, Horg, says that the leader must know how to make fire. I do not wish to be driven into the forest, like Kal. I must learn to make fire. The strangers must teach me. Otherwise they will die.'

Za strode up and down for a moment, and then turned to Hur. 'I am going to speak with the strangers again.'

'Will you ask them to show you how to make fire?'

Za nodded. 'I shall ask them many things. I shall learn from their new thoughts. I want to hear more things that I can remember.' He looked solemnly at Hur. 'A leader has many things to remember!' Using his authority as leader, Za snatched an axe from the nearest Tribesman, and headed for the cave.

In the cave of skulls, Ian, working under the Doctor's instructions, was making a kind of bow with one of his shoe-laces and a bendy piece of wood, one of the branches at the back of the cave. A long thin piece of wood, like an arrow, was wrapped in the middle of the shoe-lace.

'I hope this works, Doctor,' said Ian. 'Sure you wouldn't like to have a go?'

'No, no, young man. I merely provided the theory. The practice calls for strong wrists and unending patience, and I have neither.'

Barbara looked at the apparatus in some puzzlement. 'I still don't see how you think you're going to make fire with some kind of toy bow and arrow.'

'Easy to see you're not a science teacher,' said Ian. 'Energy into heat, remember. The idea is, I rotate the arrow bit against a chunk of dry wood, very fast and for a very long time. All my hard work gets converted into heat – and with any luck, into fire.'

'I see. The proverbial rubbing two sticks together?'

'That's right. Any boy scout is supposed to be able to do it. I only hope I can!'

Susan appeared with a flat round stone with a

hollow depression in the middle – a kind of natural bowl. 'Is this the sort of thing you want?'

'That'll do fine.'

'You'll need something very dry and tindery,' said Barbara. 'Dead leaves and old grass should do it.' She found a supply of both at the back of the cave. Carefully avoiding Old Mother's body, she carried them back.

'Good,' said Ian. 'Now, I put this bit of dry wood in the bowl, we pack the dry leaves and grass around it ... so ... and away we go!'

Ian stood the arrow in the bowl, point downwards, and held it in position with another piece of wood in his left hand. By moving the bow in his right hand backwards and forwards, he began turning the point of the arrow round and round on the flat piece of wood. He worked away steadily, and soon the point had formed a kind of groove. Round and round, moved the arrow on the piece of wood, but there was no sign of fire ...

'It's no use you all standing over me,' said Ian irritably. 'It isn't going to burst into flames straight away you know. It'll probably take all night!'

Za marched up to the sentry he had left outside the second exit from the cave. 'I go in to speak with the strange tribe. If anyone but me comes out, you will kill them.'

The tribesman nodded and Za went into the tunnel.

In the hillside immediately above the exit, there was a ledge of rock. On it lay Kal. His eyes were blazing with hatred, and the stone knife was gripped tightly in his hand.

He looked hungrily down at the unsuspecting sentry – all that stood between him and his revenge.

11

The Firemaker

Despite Ian's protests, the others were still standing round him watching his efforts. As Barbara had remarked, there wasn't really a great deal else to do in the cave, and since all their lives depended on his efforts, they could scarcely be blamed for taking an interest.

'I think I can smell something,' said Susan suddenly.

'So can I,' agreed Barbara. 'A sort of scorching . . .'

'You're doing it!' said Susan excitedly. 'It's going to work!'

Ian's forehead was dripping with sweat, and his wrists felt as if they were on fire themselves. 'Not yet,' he grunted. 'Long way . . . to go . . . yet.'

Suddenly Za appeared from the back of the cave. 'What is this? What are you doing?'

'We are making fire,' said the Doctor impressively.

('I like the "we",' thought Ian mutinously. 'Who's doing all the work?')

Za looked down at Ian. 'Friend?'

Ian looked up, stopping his work in surprise. 'What?'

'Don't stop,' said the Doctor quickly.

Hurriedly, Ian went on with his unending twirling of the stick.

'Hur said you called yourself Friend,' said Za. 'I am Za. I am leader. Are you the leader of this tribe?'

Still working, Ian glanced up at the Doctor, who was staring loftily into space.

Ian nodded towards the Doctor. 'No. He is our leader.'

'What are you going to do with us?' asked Susan anxiously. 'Are you going to set us free?'

Za looked thoughtfully at them. 'The old men of the Tribe have been talking. They say you are from Orb, the sun. They say that when you are returned to him we shall have fire again.'

'Returned? How?' asked the Doctor sharply.

'Sacrificed – on the stone of death, outside the great cave. The old men say your deaths will bring back fire.'

'But that's not true,' said Barbara horrified. 'If you kill us, you'll never have fire.'

'That is what I think,' said Za. 'I think you are a new tribe from the other side of the mountain. Show me how to make fire and I will take you back.' Za paused. 'If you do not show me how to make fire soon, I do not think I will be able to stop your dying on the stone of death.'

Ian had been toiling away all this time. Suddenly, he shouted, 'It's working. I really think

111

it's beginning to work!'

Everyone crowded round. A tiny wisp of smoke was rising from the dried grass around the flat piece of wood. 'Put some more dry grass and leaves there, Barbara. Gently though, don't smother it.'

Susan and Barbara crouched beside him, watching eagerly.

The Doctor stared imperiously at Za. 'Do you understand what we are doing? We are making fire for you.'

'I am watching.'

'The whole Tribe should be watching,' said Ian. 'Then everybody would know how to make fire.'

'Only the leader makes fire,' growled Za. 'Everybody cannot be the leader.'

'True enough – but in our tribe the firemaker is the least important man.'

'I do not believe this.'

'Oh yes,' said the Doctor loftily. 'He is the least important because in our tribe we can all make fire.'

Susan put her lips to Barbara's ear. 'I hope he doesn't make grandfather prove that!'

There was a sudden shout from Ian. 'Susan, Barbara! Blow gently just here!'

They knelt beside him and began blowing on the smouldering grass. 'Not too much,' warned Ian. 'That's right. It's glowing. There are embers there. Give me some more grass, Susan.'

By now a thin column of smoke was rising from the grass.

Suddenly there was a crackling. A flame leaped

up, and then another ...

Ian threw aside the bow and began feeding the tiny blaze with grass and twigs. The flames grew higher, higher, until a little fire was burning on the stone.

'You've done it,' shouted Susan excitedly. 'Ian, you've done it!' She threw her arms around his neck and hugged him.

Barbara patted him on the back. 'Congratulations, Ian. Well done!'

Only the Doctor did not speak. He was watching Za.

Za was gazing into the flames in utter fascination.

'Fire!' he murmured. 'Fire is back!'

Horg and the elders and the rest of the warriors were gathered around the flat-topped stone of sacrifice, talking in low voices. 'Za has been long in the cave of skulls,' said one of the warriors. 'Soon Orb will rise in the sky.'

'Za talks to the strangers,' said Hur. 'He is learning their secrets.'

'When Orb touches the stone he must bring them out,' said another. 'We shall spill their blood on the stone of sacrifice.'

'And so we wait,' grumbled Horg. 'Za talks – and we have no meat, no fruits from the trees, no roots. Za is no leader.'

'If Za could hear you speak, he would kill *you*,' said Hur angrily. '*You* would lie on the old stone till your blood runs out.'

'Perhaps Za is letting the strangers go,' said Horg suspiciously. 'Perhaps he is setting them free, as Old Mother did.'

'It is a lie,' shouted Hur. 'Za sent a warrior to watch over the cave. He told him to kill the strangers if they came out.'

But the muttering went on. Hur listened, worried. Unless Za acted soon, the Tribe would turn on him and destroy him.

The sentry outside the cave was not a very alert guard. Like all Za's people, he lacked the discipline for any prolonged task. Besides, what was the point of guarding the strangers when Za was with them?

Kal dropped from the rock above, soft-footed like a great cat, and took the guard around the throat from behind.

For a moment they stood locked in silent struggle, Kal's muscles swelling with the effort. Then the guard fell dead to the ground.

Kal drew his knife, and slipped into the tunnel that led to the cave of skulls.

The little blaze had been built up into a proper fire, blazing merrily in the centre of the cave. His brow furrowed, Za listened as Ian explained the working of the fire-bow.

The leaping flames cast giant shadows on the wall – and suddenly Susan realised that one of the shadows was not their own. A sixth shadow, huge and menacing, loomed high on the cave wall. 'Look!' screamed Susan.

They turned and saw Kal, knife in hand, advancing from the back of the cave.

Za snatched up his axe, and went to meet him.

For a moment they circled around the fire, eyeing each other, and then simultaneously, both sprang to the attack. It was a savage, brutal fight – all the more savage because soon both men lost their weapons. A lucky blow from Za's axe shattered Kal's knife to fragments. As Za raised the axe to strike, Kal sprang in beneath it, grappling with him. For a moment they struggled for possession of the axe. Suddenly Kal twisted it from Za's grasp, losing hold of it himself in the process. The axe clattered to the floor, and from then on the two men fought like wild animals with teeth and claws.

Susan buried her head on Barbara's shoulder and both looked away. Ian watched the fight with horrified fascination. The Doctor looked on dispassionately, following the progress of the battle like some Roman emperor watching two gladiators in the arena.

For some time it was hard to tell who was gaining the upper hand. Za was bulkier and stronger, but Kal was quicker and lithe as a cat. Time and time again, he twisted free from Za's hold. But Za's greater strength gave him victory in the end. Catching Kal in a terrible grip, he hurled him bodily to the ground. As Kal lay there half-stunned, Za snatched up a great rock and brought it smashing down ...

Now there was one more shattered skull in the cave of skulls.

Outside the cave, the Tribe was growing impatient. As the first rays of the sun struck the stone of sacrifice, Horg gave an angry roar. 'Orb is above us, and still there is no fire. Orb waits for his sacrifice! Call Za! Tell him to bring the strangers from out of the cave of skulls! If he does not we will sacrifice him with them!'

Za dragged Kal's body to the back of the cave, picked up his axe, and came slowly back to the fire. There was blood on his hands. 'Kal is dead now. I am leader – and we have fire!'

Suddenly there came the sound of angry shouts from outside the cave.

'Za! Za! Bring out the strangers! The strangers must be sacrificed to Orb!'

'Za! Za! Za!'

The chanting grew louder, angrier.

Ian took a long stick and lit the end in the fire. He handed it to Za. 'Here! Show this to your tribe!'

Za took the blazing branch. 'You will wait here.'

'We'll come out with you.'

'No. You will wait here!'

Holding the blazing branch high above him, Za went through the tunnel.

Angrily Ian watched him go. 'Why can't we go with him?'

'It might be safer in here,' said the Doctor. 'Let him go, Chesterton, let him go. Let him show the

Tribe fire, establish his leadership. Then he'll set us free.'

The chanting came to an instant halt when Za marched out of the cave bearing his blazing torch.

He advanced on the circle of warriors, and they shrank fearfully back. Za held out the torch. 'Fire!'

Horg stretched out his hand to the flames, and nodded reverently.

Za looked challengingly around the circle. 'Kal is dead. I give you fire. I am the leader.'

Horg bowed his head. 'Yes. You are the leader.'

'We shall give food and water to the new tribe in the cave of skulls,' ordered Za.

'There is no meat.'

Za looked at the rising sun. 'I shall go into the forest and bring back meat.'

Horg licked his lips hungrily. 'Yes. I remember how well the meat and the fire join together.'

'We shall join them again. Guard the new tribe well. They must be here when I get back. The rest of you gather wood. We shall keep the fire alive in the great cave.'

Za handed the blazing branch to Horg, and headed for the forest.

Hur watched him go, her eyes shining with pride. 'Bring fruit and water,' she ordered. 'I must feed the new tribe – as Za, the leader, commands.'

Inside the cave of skulls, the wait seemed endless. 'It didn't work,' said Ian. 'He's going to keep us here.'

117

'Someone's coming,' called Susan.

Hur came into the cave carrying fruit wrapped in a piece of skin.

'Look, what's going on?' demanded Ian. 'Why are we being kept here?'

Hur put the fruit down by the fire. 'Za has gone into the forest to hunt. Later there will be meat for you.'

'Why can't we go outside?' asked Barbara.

'Please let us go out,' pleaded Susan. 'It's terrible in here.'

'Za has ordered that you stay. Za is the leader.'

'But we helped you! We even gave you fire.'

'Yes, we have fire now,' said Hur flatly.

Hur started to move away, but Barbara caught her by the arm. 'How long have we got to stay in here? How long must we stay with you?'

'Forever,' said Hur simply. Pulling herself free, she turned and left the cave.

'We have fire now,' mimicked Ian bitterly. 'Yes, and I was the one who gave it to them – like a fool. I should have waited, bargained with them ...'

'Don't worry, my boy, you did the right thing,' said the Doctor. 'The only possible thing.'

Barbara nodded. 'At least we're still alive. We'd have been sacrificed by now if we hadn't given them fire.'

Susan looked round the gloomy cave. The light from the little fire played eerily on the shattered skulls.

'Forever,' she whispered. 'You heard what she said. They're going to keep us here forever ...'

12

Escape into Danger

Ian Chesterton woke out of a nightmare-haunted sleep, to find that the nightmare was real. He was still in the cave of skulls.

Barbara was shaking him gently by the shoulder. 'Ian, wake up. You've slept most of the day. The Doctor says it'll be dark again soon.'

Ian sat up and looked around. Susan and Barbara were sitting beside him, and the Doctor was adding branches to the fire.

'They've brought us some meat,' said Susan. 'I think it's supposed to be cooked.' She pointed to a leaf on which were a few chunks of charred and bloody meat.

'There's some water too,' said Barbara, 'in a kind of hollow stone. We saved you some.'

'All the comforts of home, eh?'

She passed Ian a kind of natural stone bowl, and he sipped the water thirstily. 'I don't think I'll bother with the meat.'

'I shouldn't,' said Barbara. 'It isn't very nice.'

Ian looked at the Doctor, who sat gazing blankly into the fire. He looked tired and dispirited.

They heard movement from the back of the cave.

Za appeared from the gloom. He marched up to the fire and stood looking down at them. 'You have meat now.'

No one answered.

'The animal was strong and hard to kill, but I killed it. Now there is meat for all the Tribe. The meat is good.'

More silence.

'They have brought you fruit and water in a hollow stone.' Za looked down. 'Is this the stone?'

'He's trying to make conversation,' thought Barbara hysterically.

Za seemed puzzled, almost hurt by their lack of response. 'Has anyone hurt you?'

The Doctor raised his head. 'When are you going to let us go?'

'You will stay here,' said Za flatly. 'I have the thing that you made, but I do not know if it will make fire for me. It will be best if your tribe and my Tribe join together – forever.'

'No,' shouted Ian angrily. 'We want to leave here!'

'Why? The cave is warm and dry. We will bring you food and water and wood to feed the fire. There is no better place on the other side of the mountains.' Menacingly, Za raised his axe. 'Do not try to leave here – or you will die!'

He turned and strode from the cave.

Ian found a sharp stick, speared a piece of meat, looked at it in disgust and pitched it into the fire, where it sizzled angrily.

The Doctor said moodily. 'Fire! Fire is still the answer, somehow, I'm sure of it. They revere it! If only we could use it to frighten them in some way.' He kicked moodily at a skull at his feet. It rolled into the fire, sat there, grinning at him.

'Look at that skull, grandfather,' said Susan fearfully. 'It looks almost alive.'

Inside the empty eye-sockets of the skull, little flames flickered like glaring eyes.

Ian looked at the skull, and then jumped to his feet. 'Not alive, Susan – dead! Get me some pieces of wood, will you? We're going to make some torches – we can use the fat from the meat. Doctor, see if you can find me four skulls, not too badly bashed up.'

'What happens then?' asked Susan.

'Then to all intents and purposes, we're going to be dead. Just like that skull!'

Ian pointed to the fast-blackening skull in the heart of the fire.

The Tribe was having a great feast that night, sitting round the huge fire that roared at the mouth of the main cave. They crowded around it, roasting chunks of bloody meat on the end of sticks, thrusting them into their mouths when they were no more than charred. Children munched and played in the circle of firelight. Their mothers looked on, with no fear that the beasts from the forest would snatch them away.

Za sat in the place of honour, flanked by Hur on one side, Horg on the other. He looked proudly around his Tribe. They were warm, well fed, and safe – and he was their chief.

Suddenly there came a terrible cry of fear and a Tribesman ran into the circle of firelight.

Za jumped to his feet in anger. 'You were told to guard the strangers. Why are you here?'

The man was almost sobbing with fear. 'I was waiting outside the tunnel when I heard the stranger tribe calling me. There was a great wailing and shouting, so I crept to the end of the passage to look . . . There has been great magic, Za. You must come and see.'

'Show me,' ordered Za. 'The men will come with me, the rest stay here.' He ran towards the cave of skulls, Horg and the warriors at his heels. Hur ran after them.

The trembling guard led the way to the side entrance and pointed. He would go no further. Za marched into the little tunnel, followed by Hur, Horg and his warriors.

As they came into the cave, a horrifying sight met their eyes. The stranger tribe had vanished. In their place hovered four gleaming skulls, flames burning from their eyes, and belching out from their mouths.

Horg fell to his knees in terror. 'The strangers have died! Their ghosts have come to punish us.'

The rest of the Tribe fell to their knees, wailing in fear.

Even Za stood frozen with terror, staring fixedly at the skulls.

In the shadows at the back of the cave, Ian

122

whispered, 'Right, let's slip out now. Hurry!'

One by one they edged round behind the terrified Tribesmen, and down the tunnel that led to freedom. No one saw them – all eyes were on the four skulls. Seconds later, they were outside in the cold night air. Nearby they could see frightened figures huddled round the great fire outside the main cave. Keeping well away from the firelight, they ran into the forest.

One of the skull-bearing torches was almost burned away. Suddenly it collapsed beneath the weight of its burden and the charred skull rolled almost to Za's feet.

The others leaped back in fear, but Za shouted, 'Look! This is nothing but fire and the bones of the dead!'

He snatched up one of the torches, shaking free the skull, and held it high, looking around the cave. 'The stranger tribe have gone. While we looked at their fire and cried with terror before dead bones, they have gone!'

'They have gone into the night,' said Hur. 'The dark will hide them.'

Za waved his torch in a flaming circle. 'With fire, night is day,' he said grimly. 'Bring fire all of you. We shall hunt them down!'

He led the way outside the cave and selected a band of his best warriors. Armed with blazing torches, the hunters set off at a run.

Ian led his little party through the forest at top

speed. This time no one had any difficulty in keeping up. Even the Doctor didn't demand that they stop and rest.

They fled blindly through the darkness, and Ian hoped desperately that they were still on the right path.

It was with a feeling of enormous relief that he led them at last into the clearing where Za had fought the tiger. 'Nearly there,' he gasped.

They heard fierce yells behind them, and turning round they saw the gleam of fiery torches through the trees.

'Quick,' yelled Ian. 'They're right behind us! Run!'

They forced their way out of the forest at a stumbling run, bursting through the screen of bushes, and out onto the sandy plain.

The going was easier now, and a few more minutes brought them to the TARDIS.

Ian collapsed against the door, and turned to the Doctor, who was bringing up the rear. 'Hurry, Doctor, let us in. They'll be here any minute!'

The Doctor staggered up, fumbled for the key with agonising slowness, got the door open at last, and tumbled inside.

Ian ushered Barbara and Susan through the door, and turned for a last look behind him. He saw Za and his warriors burst out of the forest and onto the plain. One of the warriors hurled a spear, which clattered against the TARDIS.

Ian dashed inside and the doors closed behind him. 'Come on, Doctor, get us out of here!'

The Doctor was already busy at the controls ...

Za skidded to a halt in frustration, before the strange blue tree. Za glared angrily at it. 'Smash it down,' he roared. He dashed at the strange object, axe raised high. The thing gave a strange wailing cry – and disappeared. Everyone flung themselves to the ground in terror. The thought came into Za's terrified mind that he had been wrong – surely the strangers did come from Orb after all.

It was some time later. Rested and refreshed, Ian and Barbara and Susan watched the Doctor anxiously as he hovered over the controls, making a rapid series of adjustments.

The central column slowed its rise and fall, and the Doctor looked up. 'I think the co-ordinates are matching ... yes, they're definitely matching.' He sounded rather surprised.

'Good,' said Susan. She smiled at the others. 'We'll be landing soon.'

'Where?' asked Ian suspiciously.

The Doctor sighed. 'How I wish I knew!'

'Aren't you taking us back?'

'Now, how can I do that? Do be reasonable.'

'But please,' said Barbara. 'You must take us back. You must!'

The Doctor tapped the central control console. 'The trouble is,' he said confidentially. 'This thing isn't really working properly! What's more, part of its code is still a secret.' He looked sternly at Ian. 'However, given the right data, precise informa-

ون as to the time and place of the *beginning* of a journey, a *destination* can be fixed. But when we left, I had no such data at my disposal.'

Barbara looked at him in horror. 'Do you mean to tell me you don't really know how all this works? And what's more, you don't even know where we've arrived?'

'Precisely,' said the Doctor, apparently in answer to both questions. He turned away in a huff, muttering, 'Really! Do they think I'm a miracle-worker?'

'You can't blame grandfather,' said Susan protectively. 'We left the other place too quickly, that's all. We never did find out exactly where and when we were!'

The central column was moving slower and slower now; finally, it came to a complete halt. 'We've arrived,' said the Doctor.

'Just a minute,' said Ian. 'You did try to get us back to our own time, didn't you, Doctor?'

'I got you away from that other time, young man.'

'That wasn't what I asked you.'

'It's the only way I can answer you.' The Doctor turned away and switched on the scanner.

The landscape it showed seemed bare and lifeless.

'Not much of an improvement,' said Ian.

'I agree,' said the Doctor briskly. 'Could be anywhere!'

'What do we do now?'

'There's only one thing we can do. Go outside

the ship and try to obtain our precise temporal and spatial co-ordinates – that is, if you want me to get you home again.' The Doctor rubbed his hands. 'Radiation count, Susan?'

Susan tapped the dial. 'Seems to be zero, grandfather.'

'Good. Then we can go out and find out where we are.'

Ian looked at Barbara. She nodded.

'Lead the way, Doctor,' said Ian resignedly.

The Doctor opened the doors and went outside. Susan followed.

Ian took Barbara's arm. 'Well – here we go again!'

They went outside, and the door closed behind them.

Unseen, the dial on the radiation counter flickered into life. Like so much of the TARDIS's equipment, it tended to be erratic, and Susan's tap had started it working again. The needle swung slowly across the dial, until it entered the section marked 'Danger'.

Although the Doctor and his companions were not yet aware of it, they were heading into even greater danger. The planet on which they had landed was called Skaro and it had been devastated by years of warfare between two races, the Kaleds and the Thals.

Over the long years of warfare, the Kaleds had changed, mutated even, building themselves war machines in which to live and fight. They had changed their name as well as their appearance.

The Doctor was about to meet the creatures who were destined to become his greatest enemies.

Out there on Skaro, the Daleks were waiting for him.